The Secret of the Cicadas' Song

a peyote trip in prose and poetry

by

Michael Lyons

HiT MoteL Press
www.hitmotel.com

Copyright 1998 by Michael Lyons
All rights reserved.
First Edition

Library of Congress Cataloging in publication Data

Lyons, Michael
        The Secret of the Cicadas' Song
I. Title

ISBN: 0-9655842-1-6

Published by HiT MoteL Press

Designed by Michael Lyons

To Mother

The clearest way to get into the Universe
is to walk through a forest.
--John Muir

The Secret of the Cicadas's Song

part 1

Hyperspectral / the Dirac Satori

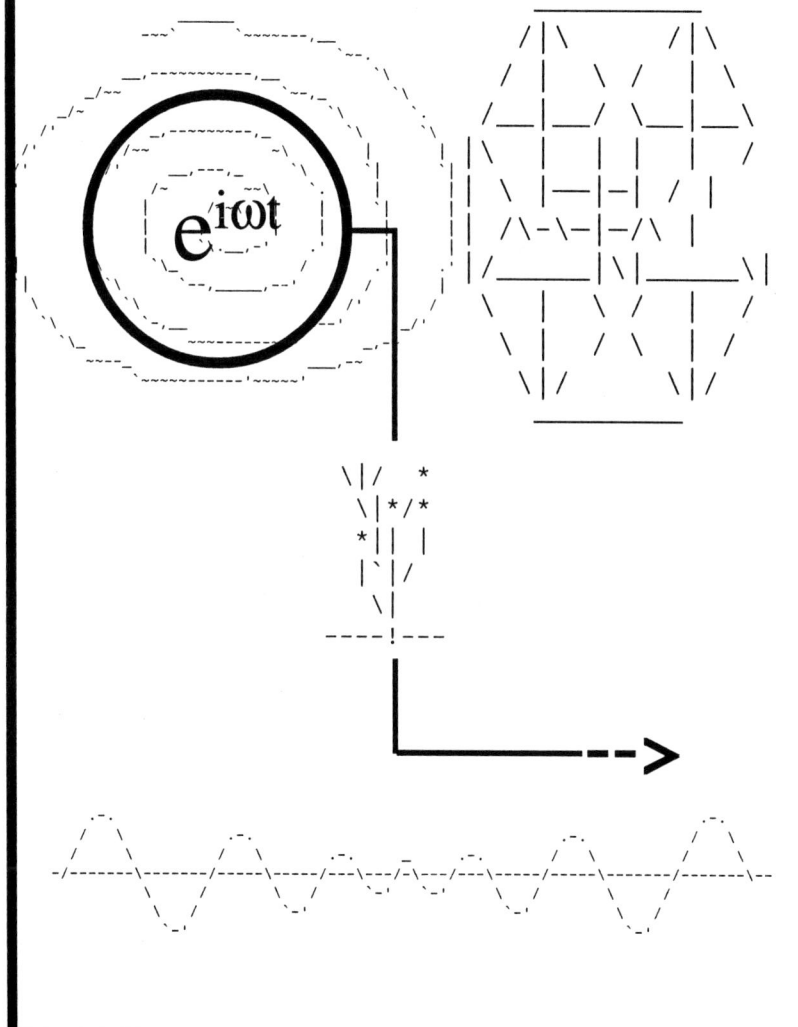

The Secret of the Cicadas' Song

Hyperspectral / the Dirac Satori

Hyperspectral / the Dirac Satori	1
begining (chirping vs ululating)	8
dead philosopher	8
Onset of Satori	10
Mondrian	15
Stockhausen	18
fretwork	20
The Secret of the Cicadas' Song	22
eXplosion, transcendental	26
a potential entelechy	30
the semiotics of symbiosis	34
Think of Something Big — Nature at Play	38
surrealism blows away boundaries	39
peyoteros must change the names of things	41
The name of the wind	43
What would René say	46
The Tree of Life	56
Peyote Sings	68

Gaia and the Green Bank

I seem to be a fractal in the Green Bank	78
relativity	79
leaf feather	91
Green Bank parade	92
Green Bank as recursive, acausal, semi-permeable membrane	93
a bit of a bummer	95
she, Gaia, when	102
Oxygen	105
the floating brain,	106
Mushrooms	107
The DNA computer	109
where does language begin / the real name of water	113
Green Bank formula	121
Green Bank Definition	125
the heart is a strange attractor	126
The Background Hiss of Summer	130

Hyperspectral / The Dirac Satori
an alternative version of
The Background Hisss of Summer
Chapter 13 of the novel
Cultivating the Texas Twister Hybrid

Ruth had brought a bag of peyote buttons out with her. It was cool to eat peyote out at the farm because you felt safe, isolated. Wasn't anybody going to be coming up that road. Besides, the gate was locked, they'd need the combination. You could get totally whacked out of your skull.

I started feeling nervous when she placed the dried-up gnarly-looking cactus apples on the table. I remembered the horrendous taste, and how you always have to barf your guts out before you see God. Another thing is, I didn't usually like to trip with anybody. You have to really trust the person you're gonna trip with and I trusted nobody. Least of all lovers. Also I am a day tripper, I didn't like to trip at night. So, though I was intimidated, I was thankful, at least, that we would be tripping during the day. I ate a little, enough to be sociable, enough to get high but not enough to, go over to the edge.

We smoked a little tea to take the nauseating alkaline taste out of our mouths and to tide us over until the hallucinogen came on. Ruth did a ritual, wafting burning cedar incense into the four corners. The marijuana smoke mixed with the cedar incense and floated up into the still air. We started to make some conversation to bridge the silence.

"Have you noticed," Ruth began, "that there is a big difference between the sounds of the grasshoppers at night and during the day. During the day they are really loud."

"That's for damn sure," I said. " People who grow up around this all their lives, it must either drive them nuts or it must do something to their brains, get their minds aligned or something."

"I think," she said, "they rub, as they sit there. They rub their legs together..."

"Yeah that's the uh, stridulating," I interjected. "It's called stridulating, I read it in the book you got."

"Yeah," she offered tenuously agreeing.

"And they rub that big hairy legs across their wings," I continued. We listen in to the caterwauling of all the katydids. "It's like a bowed instrument."

"Ahh," she said.

"And the reason why the crickets and cicada sounds are different during the day and at night," I told her, "is because they are tied to the temperature. I read in the book the other day you can compute the actual temperature from the sounds they make. If you count the number of chirps in 14 seconds and you add 42 to it, you get the actual temperature."

"I don't believe you," she teased. "You're making that up."

"No, that's what it says."

We listened to the staccato caterwauling of the cicadas and the crickets all a jumble in the hisss of the summer's day.

"I don't know how they count it though," I said.

We both were listening intently. Cicada was loud. The sound was endless, and it wavered and shifted as if there were varying pockets of density in space. At times it seems like the insects were making a concerted effort to fracture a wall or pierce some kind of veil with their endless sound beams.

"How do you count chirps in that?" I asked. "You must have to have an oscilloscope of something."

She looked thoughtful for a moment. "Do you have a watch with a second hand?"

"No, I don't even have a watch. But I can count seconds."

"All right let's give it a try," she said

"OK."

"Number of chirps in 14 seconds," she said.

"OK. Ready. Set. Go." I said.

There didn't seem to be any break or discrete bursts in the wall of sound washing over them.

"Oh it's impossible," Ruth said. "My god."

"How do they come up with that. I wonder," I said.

"Do you think they could like slow it down or something? Oh, my god," she said.

"They must have to record it and play it back," I said.

"Or maybe if you just start like on a cold day," she said.

"Or maybe," I said, "they just mean the whole burst. It's 14 bursts of chirps, like these are really long because these are day crickets. Or maybe at night they are not so close together and shorter."

"All right I'm gonna give it another try," she said. "Tell me when it's time."

"All right I'll start counting 1001, 1002, 1003, ...That's 14 seconds. How many chirps?"

"The way I figured it out if I can just go like this," she said and she raised her hand and brought it down like a maestro giving the down stroke, "It's like there's 5 chirps every time I go like that."

"Oh, yeah. Estimate. Good." I said.

So as I was counting, she was raising and lowering her hand abruptly. "I don't know. I think I got 45. So what would that be?" She asked.

"Well then 45 and 42 would make it about 87 degrees," I said. "It's about right."

"Let's go over to the porch. Lets look at the thermometer." She walked up onto the back porch and read it of.

"89 degrees! Not bad."

"Yeah pretty close."

"Damn, they've really got it down to a science don't they," she said kind of disappointed, with a kind of sadness for something that had just been quantified out of mystery.

"Yep. The sound that the crickets and the cicadas make is directly related to the temperature," I said with scientific certitude.

'Yeah like I said, Mr. Know-it-All, the hotter it gets the louder they get."

"Yeah but now with the Cicada," I mused, "you don't have discrete chirps that you can count. Here we have continuous white noise trilling. We'd have to do some kind of harmonic analysis to find the mean frequency."

Ruth gave me that kind of glazed-over bewildered stare I had seen often enough in my life. Oh, oh, I am slipping into science again. I was starting to feel nauseated and rushy.

Beginning

"It would be like trying to find the mean frequency of the back ground hiss of summer." I mumbled. The itchy restlessness was setting in — upsetting body sensations were running up and down the back of my neck.

"Listen Ruth, I'm gonna take a little walk-about and check on the patch. I'll be back in a little while." I had never invited Ruth to the patch. I wanted to make sure she was innocent of all that —in case they captured and tortured her. Besides my partner had forbade it.

I arose creakily and headed back into the animal pens. I worried about leaving her all by her lonesome, but she was used to it I'm sure my eyes looked wild. One eye looks out and the other looks in. There was just so much to explore rather than give your attention to one person.

There was some kind of struggle between Ruth and me. A friendly but gut-wrenching battle of archetypes, the mother and the father, the lovers. God I hope she didn't want to have sex, that was the last thing on my mind. When I have psychedelics I can't perform to save my soul. On psychedelics I became a philosopher and a mystic and was like as not to cogitate in public (cogitate cogitate, throw up all the food you ate.) I could sense a hollowness within, a tunnel opening up. My first priority was not whether but where I was going to barf. I didn't need anyone to hold my head.

Along with my fiery guide dog, Blake,

I took my green colored
        personage

into the green hell of the afternoon heat.

    Green hills,
             green wind.
The cicadas were really drilling into the summer sun.

The constant
    incessant

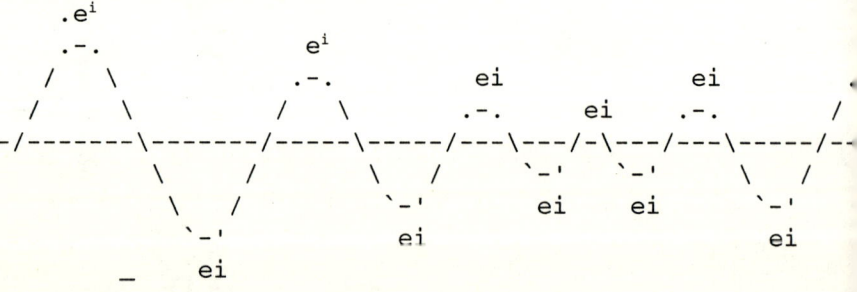

                rock drill

of the cicadas

above
the
crick crick crack crack ....cika cika cika crick crick
layer of the crickets beneath.

It has a strangely calming effect.

It better, either that or it will drive you mad.
It billows out all around you
like the sides of the tent

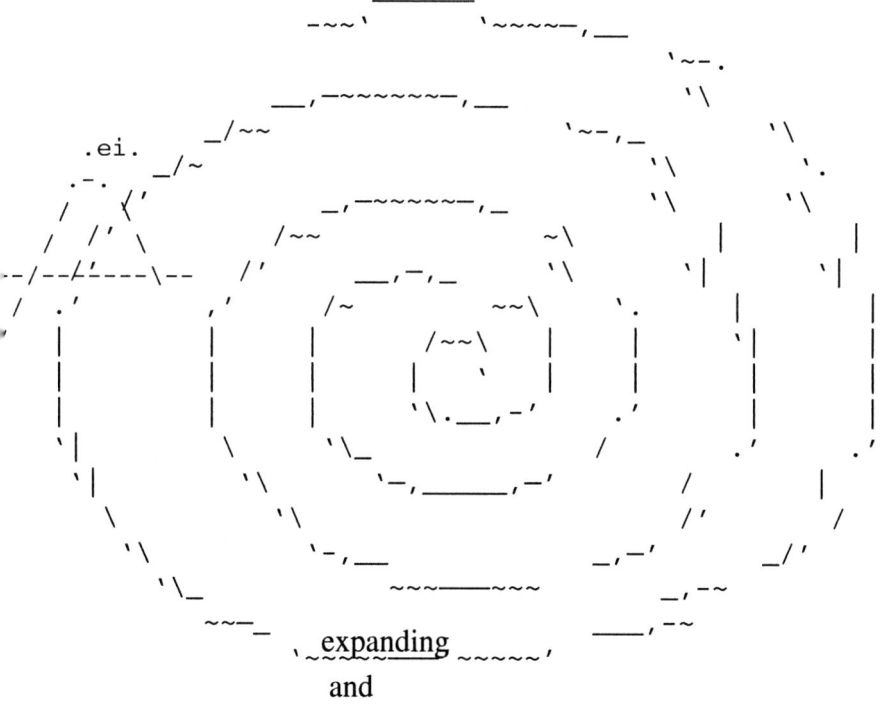

expanding
and
contracting on the breeze.

dead philosopher

I am stumbling
               toward the manifold.

    My mind is agitated and I'm in a paranoid sweat as I do the snake shuffle through the dried reeds and dead weeds toward the patch. I could spend years rotting in prison for husbanding this illegal weed.

    SCENE FROM ABOVE
    it is completely still
    I am leaving the house
    there is no one
    there's not a cloud in the sky
    it just goes on and on
    like an immense swimming pool I could dive into
    an entire planet with no one on it
    except for a lowly peon in white
    shuffling along a path
    being toyed with by the jeering sneering blearing sun
    making everything prickly with heat

    I was wearing loose white cotton and a big wide brimmed Panama.
    I had more of a body awareness. If a tick or any insect got on me, I could immediately sense it and gracefully, absent-mindedly remove the critter.
    Being always alert for snakes, led to a kind of enhanced awareness of the environment.

    I could see my obituary notice in the Daily Texan:

Snake-Bitten Philosopher Dies

The white clad body of philosopher Walker Underwood was found in a field outside Manor. He was on a walk with his dog, when bitten by a rattlesnake. The wool-gathering graduate student of the University of Texas, who many said had been struck by god, was thought to have been distracted and not heeding the snake's hissing warning signs.

Underwood is remembered as a regular in the Student Union and other places on campus for holding forth in spontaneous public address.

"I remembered thinking what a lost soul he was," said friend Jules Windish. "He was the fool on the hill. He always wore white to identify with the working class peon. I had to admire his ideas and for trying to turn the university into a Platonic agora in which men openly and earnestly discussed philosophy and religion."

I stumble
    and crash to the ground!
        don't roll!
  (there might be snakes.)
        try to get up!
not the slightest movement
down here close to the ground
    snakes curl and slither
    amid the hollows

I see my empty hand reaching
    as I struggle to get up
and the tree beyond it reaching

(breeze in the line of trees along the creek)
    WAVES take SHAPE in the FIELDS
      ~~~~~~~~~~~~~~~~~~~
      ~~~waves~~~~~~~~~~~
      ~~~~~~~~~waves~~~~~~~
      ~~~~~~~~~~~~~~~~~~~~

and there was no way to stop it,
and upon my hands and knees
I leaned over and barfed my guts out
    bla!
        bla!
           bleah!
Afterwards I let out a loud
    HAAAH,
sigh of relief.
Looking up from the second hand peyote at the sun I knew this was going to be a big one.

Onset of Satori

then I look up
and see grasshopper sitting on a branch.
Its face is green and smooth,
blunt and shiny as a motorcycle helmet.
I find myself
    kneeling
before
an automaton,
a robot,
a living machine.

I remember just looking at it.
I am quiet
he is stridently chirping
by rubbing his big hairy leg across his thorax.

over
and over
again

he does it.
rapidly.

he is looking at me as if he is masturbating in public.

I became fixated on the entity
this machine/being
this leaping, green space-vehicle,
this light assault vehicle
tied to the mother ship.

And even though I was afraid of snakes
I stayed down on my knees,
marveling at this strange fruit
and thinking
it's *watching* me.

Suddenly I could see myself through its eye!
the many faceted compound eye

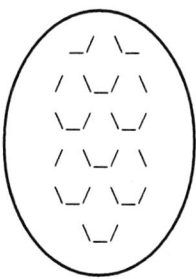

of the grasshopper

grasshopper leaped
a dolor sinks down into me
                      deep
          deep
           deep
             deep
               deep
                   deep
                       deep
                           deep
                             deep

```
                              _   _
                             / \_/ \
                             \_/ \_/
                                       _
                                      / \
                                      \_/
                                           _____
                                       ___/
                                       \__
                                          \__
```

you are going to sleep
       only to dream up the other
              world and
              be set free to
              run wild
              in it

Crickets were bowing their resonance cavities
in the hollows of the tall grass
drawing from the moving heat,
inspiration to jam with the white noise.

I begin to listen:

[CRICK CRICK CRICK CRICK CRICK] ...

       against the piercing white noise of the cicada.

There was a long pause

in which

        an uncorrolated fluctuation

propagated

                —across

        the thermal medium...

and in the pause between call and response,

(my 3D hearing mechanism kicks in
and I am listening
to an echo,)
    from little
    zephyr rivulets
    of snaking thermal curl,
        backwash
        and laminar flow
            --turbulence and scurry
                  at the edge of the field,
it was answered.
CHI CH] ... [CH CH CH] ... [CH] ... [CH CH] ... [CH] ... [CH CH] ... [CEI].

their sound is like the twinkling of stars
        they twinkle at each other

It was a blessed day for my first satori
and I then fell into a despair

    tears began to fill my eyes,

    the space between us became all blurry with water,

I knew I was feeling all this despair
because of the immensity of this intelligence
coming across infinite space
    sweeping
        down through the clouds
           around this world
        to this point
        onto the Texas prairie
    stretching forward and flat as far as the eye could see
and I knew
I could never create anything so perfect.

And I am sitting there
with green greasing my chin,
feeling awful and wonderful
looking
 at the prototype type machine
calling
    across
        space

and getting answered!

Mondrian

I stagger up and move in the direction of the pot patch.
Come!
we are drifting
        dispersing
        there
    toward the manifold
      the (hue)manifold
the trees flourish into colors all florid and chromatic
as if a mad painter had gone through
hitting each bush
with his brush
making it like a speaker
"playing" its color out of its mouth of shadows.
it is dazzling,
shifting into iridescent bright
then softening to skin of the lily white
    THE PLANES OF THE PENS
    The animal pens are leaning this way and that,
    their corrugated siding waving up and sideways,
    perpendicular and parallel planes.
    And here and there cylindrical fence poles.

    The dry fields beyond are a warm brown shot through with yellows. The yellow blurs, like when a film slips out of its sprockets and gets stuck in the lens, the light burning through it, melting around the edges curling the frame to reveal the machinery moving the film.
    "Oh oh, the frame is slipping," I thought.

LET THE EXPERIMENTS CONTINUE

the Vedic experiments:
I do the peripheral vision experiment
going walleyed

to slow time down in the edge of vision,

the vision seems to be tunneling,

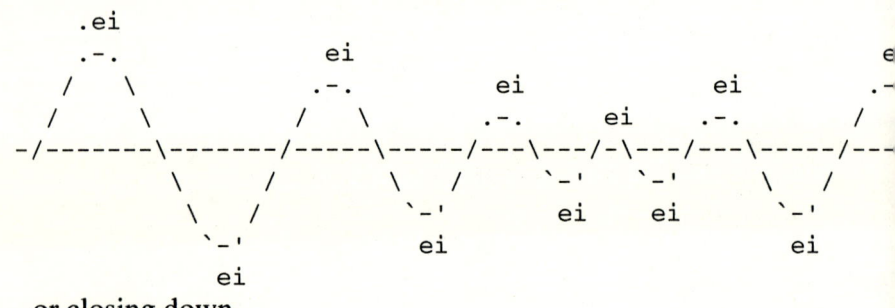

or closing down
the shadowy world
 behind the surface of things
         is machinating,
and you can change time and see it.

the peyote is giving these golden harmonics
shot through
         with green
                 and red that can be read

in the periphery.

Mondrian knew
He was trying to get his hand
on the space/time manifold, --the field
looking beyond the surfaces of planes,
beyond the blurs of color,
trying to follow the lines of sound
into the manifold
trying to bring some formality to the chaos,

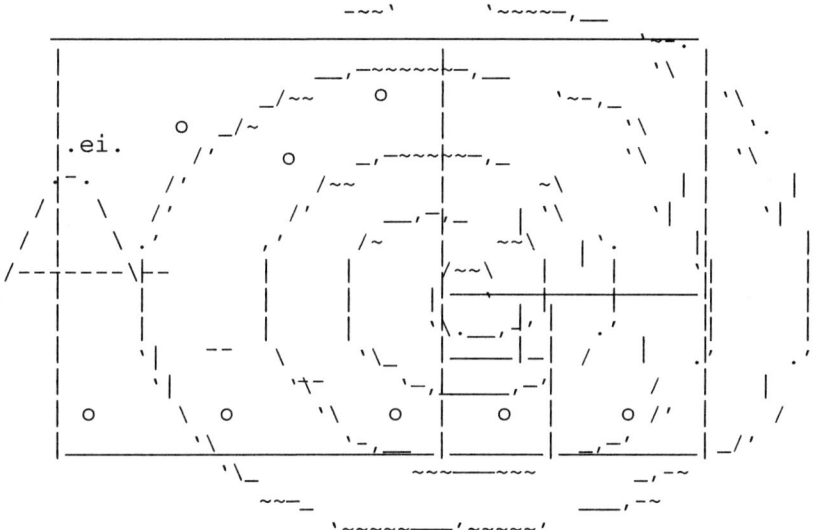

Fields.
We understand fields by an analogy to our atmosphere:
just as our atmosphere, while invisible to the eye,
supports visible phenomena like clouds,
storms   birds,   so too there is
an Original Universe of Pure Neumenal Energy
a Proto-atmosphere which supports phenomena
an invisible Universal Manifold of Space/Time
through which
potentialities must emerge into actualities.

Stockhausen

I am stumbling
toward the manifold,
the surroundings are shifting
> purple red white orange
> sound motion
>> breeze through stillness,

when I stop, I don't make a sound
 a natural stalking technique.
I listen....
and I hear...
> everything

sounds, colors, movements, electric fields, waves, heat

they got this rhythm going,
it is a droning didgeriedo,
with some high pitched crickets working around it.
like the weather around the jet stream
males competing on a front.

the pastoral symphony—NOT
but a much more modern thing
full of angst and scientific wonder
full of motion and phase shifting and the voices.
I think of Stockhausen

I am staggering along
I can barely function
I am out here because I am
trying to apply an ancient method from the Vedas
updated through Kant's Critique of Transcendental Knowledge
to understand the manifold.
and I think to get some insight from
the Stockhausen's notation.

```
 |-|            |  |-| |       |+|  |+|    |   |-| |      |+|  |+|
-|   |- - - -  |-|-|++++|+|+|  |+++|-|-|=|=|   |+++|
 |-|           |=|-|=|          |+|  |+|       |
```

It is a kind of multi-track notation, moving along in time.
It is the score of the great Ambient Composer.

+ higher OR louder OR longer OR more segments
- lower OR softer OR shorter OR fewer segments
= same (similar) register AND dynamics AND durations AND timbre AND number of segments
wow, there is a lot in that.

I think to look through it for the Moment.
and maybe catch a glimpse of the Ambient Composer.
crick crick crack ....cika cika cika crick crick crack
.. millions...shift swell...drop off over here ...shape shift..swirl leaf's smoke....vibrate sensibilities... live so hard... blast sound .... become sound.... become blots on radar.... infrared rareties... moving through the field....cika cika cika
crick crick crack ....cika cika cika crick crick crack

fretwork

somewhat later I saw, shadow like Gratings
running through the field of vision

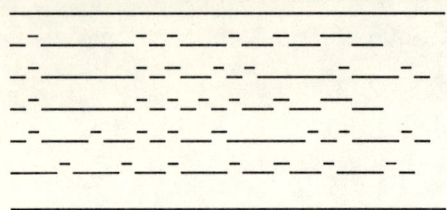

it was probably the way the strident cicada sound
was grating on my nerves
an incessant play of filigreed colors.
in the wavering shimmering shifting frieze
I saw a lattice of yellow-greens horizontal stripes
ornamental fretwork
it drifted over and enveloped me
i tried to run, through the pampas

```
          -     o
          -    <!-
          -  -\/\
          -      \
```

I was so zonked i could see the vapor trails
artifacts of my slowed down perception coming off my movement

in the moment

then i realized that i am in the grating
    I am fretwork;

I hear what I am seeing,
I think what I am smelling; everything is fretwork....
I am music,
I am climbing in music;
      HHHHaaaaaa
  la la la la la la la la la la la
    eeeeeeeeeeeeeeeeeeeeeeeeeee

  tried to match the pitch of the cicadas which was very high, while at the same time do it in rhythm with the crickets, or at lease the rhythm of the crickets that I could discern

  there appeared to be a brown Spiral, a wide band revolving madly around the axis of sight. the band spiral opens and closes as a concertina according to the rhythm of the whistling whereby bright light falls through the intermediate spaces

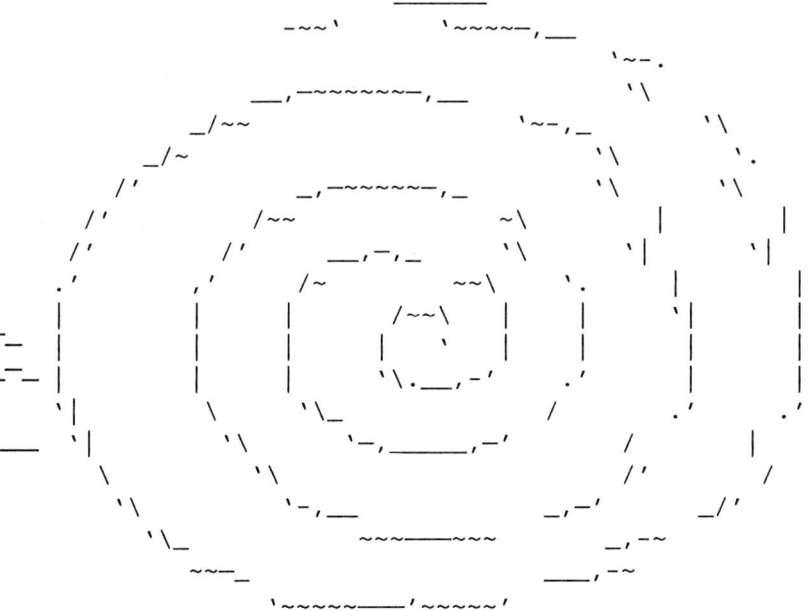

The Secret of the Cicadas' Song

Actually it was the fireflies,
that first brought me into the presence
of a strange attractor.
Yes it was the
summer night fireflies
settling in along a tree bough.

At first they just seemed to be flashing randomly.
Soon however
      small clumps of them began to flash together
and I watched in amazement
as this synchronization began to spread
until finally the whole swarm is flashing in unison.
I half expected to see them coalesce into a sign
a flashing marquee which might say coca-cola or
RCA or something.
it might say:
we are aware of each others,
and we like to dance in unison.

each little firefly
turning on and off
was like a little oscillator,
and these fireflies
had become phase-locked oscillators!

in school, we studied this.
They were like heart cells,
Each firefly influences his neighbors by
the feedback of repeated signals so that an oscillator closest to
its firing threshold senses a signal from its neighbor and it fires
off immediately.

At that point oscillators become locked together.
This process continues until all the fireflies become coupled
They form self-organizing waves.

~~~~~~~~~~~~~~~~~~~~
~~~waves~~~~~~~~~~~
~~~~~~~~~~waves~~~~~~
~~~~~~~~~~~~~~~~~~~~~

I though something like this might be going on with the cicadas too.

I had been driven mad
    by their incessant eieeieieie
        all summer
rising and falling like sheets
    blowin' in the wind.

But that is only their time series:
the high frequency of the individual cicadas' oscillations
on fast time scales
    within
an oscillating envelope on a slower time scale.
--Classical phase modulation.

it wasn't till I got up on the roof, and got the whole sense of the toroidal attractor in the background hiss of summer
that I got it.

the ambient rarefactions and phase shifting soundscape of the forest
seemed to go AROUND and around like I was somehow in a kind of phase music, a kind of lissajous merry-go- round.

I had climbed up on the roof of the house to keep an eye out for the federales and rustlers. Since the roof made an L, it was just a nice angle

It was gorgeous this quasi periodic undulating soundscape.
up high you are surrounded on all sides
by the periodic variation of many incommensurate frequencies,
which in the phase space of my hearing mechanism, traced out
the surface of a "doughnut."
AND I WAS IN THE HOLE!

It WAS like listening to a lisajoux figure!
and with my audio mechanism I had detected my first strange
attractor in phase space.

I was awestruck,
        simply awestruck.
I felt like one of the little lemurs
those night gremlins who lived right around the time
of the dinosaurs and who evolved this tremendous sense of
hearing
it was there that
from having to locate things in a space of hearing,
in a night jungle so dark you couldn't see anything anyway,
that they had to develop maps of their surroundings,
and that was how consciousness started,
from the audile brain locating sounds in space
and making a mental construct of that space
and holding it in memory.

and it was important
because it was the first time
that an animal moved
from episodic memory
to semiotic memory.

Some of the Archetypes of Perception

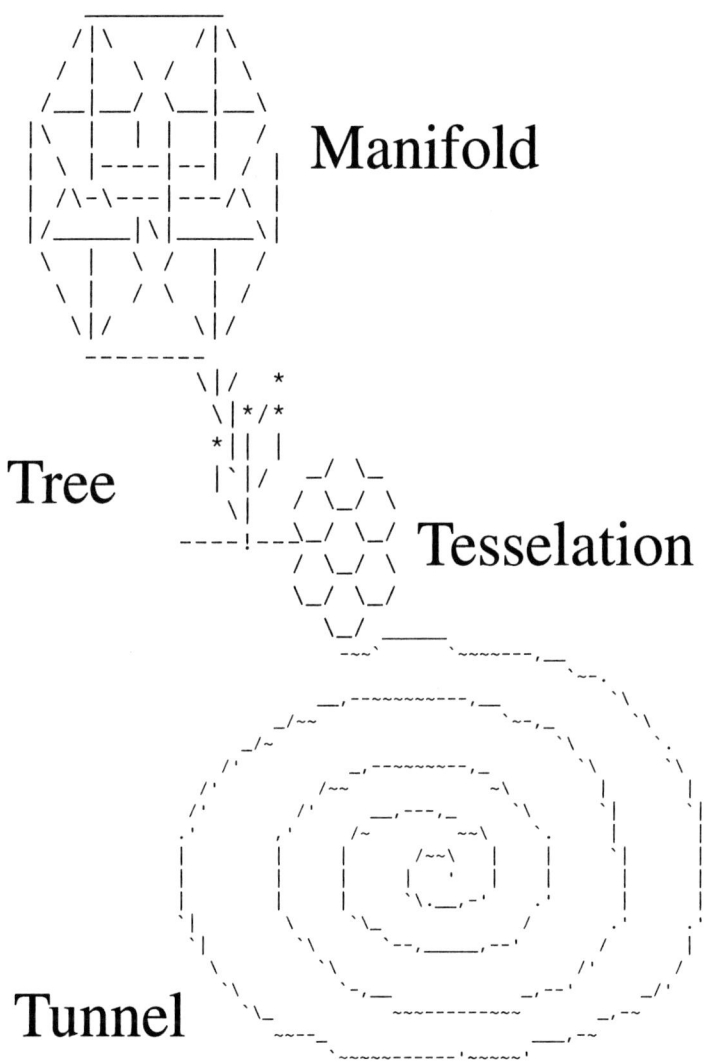

eXplosion, transcendental

My God,
and I am (listening)there
                ))) listening (((
    (0) (o)   (o)))))o(((((

The cicada high pitched trill going wild
    eeeieieieieeeeii above the
        crick crick crack crack ....cika cika cika crick crick
layer of the crickets beneath.

$e^i\ e^i\ \ e^i\ e^i\ e^i$
that's how i heard it and saw it
like e the transcendental number
base of the natural logarhytm
raised to the exponential of i, the imaginary number
going off in all directions.

```
           /   \./   \/\_                      /\       /\      /\/\/\/\/\/\/\.-.-
        __{!\_ _eⁱ_    )    eⁱ/!\         /  \   /  \   /
       /   /\_/!\._eⁱ_/   //   /─────────/    \_/    \_/
      (   (__{(@)eⁱ\__eⁱ.//_/__                                        ____--
       \__/{/(_)\_eⁱ    )\\ \\-                                    ____---
         (    (__)_)_/   )\ \>─────────────────────
          \__/       \__/\/\/
             \__,--'
```

                              the Number

                                   e

                          transcendental as the Spirit
                          bergoining and exploding and
                          diffusing and suffusing
                          and diverging and curling

going off in all directions.
                                      $e^{\,i(x,y,z)}$

We need to break it down into its components

$e^i \quad e^i \quad e^i \quad e^i \quad e^i$

or taking out the cumbersome rectangular coordinates and reducing it to the polar coordinates in the plane

$e^{i\emptyset} \quad e^{i\emptyset} \quad e^{i\emptyset} \quad e^{i\emptyset} \quad e^{i\emptyset} \quad e^{i\emptyset}$

we get a sweeping cone of attention
the light cone

explosion

                transcendental
Language

listen into the Big ambient cosmic line noise
?   ?crick X   SEX   ?crick tXsha   ??shaXX   ?tX
crick XX X?t crick crick X ?   sha?   sha ?%X   crick   ?crick crick crick sha?
?crick crick Xcrick   ?%
XXcrick crick crick XX X? Xcrick shaXX ?X crick shaX   XX   crick crick
crick crick crick crick X   ? tXcrick XX
   crick crick crick crick crick crick crick XX? ?   ??%   ? XXcrick XXcrick ?   crick shaX
?tX   ?crick %shaX   ??crick crick shaSEX ??
─────────crick crick X crick crick ?   ?tX   SEX   ?XX   ?XX   ????
   XX   \⁷⁄₂?crick sha ?· · · ·─── shacrick crick shaX   ? shaX   ??
shaX ?crick shaX   crick crick sha\ erick crick XX   Xcrick XX?   crick crick
crick crick X? shaSEX   ?crick   crick sha
─ ─ ─ ─ ─ ? ?\HHH/ ?crick   crick shacrick crick XX ?   ??crick crick crick
crick crick crick crick ?crick shashashaXX
Scrick crick shaXXtshaX   ???crick XX?   ?crick crick XX   ?   crick crick crick
crick shashaX   ?? tSEXXX
     ?   SEX   Xcrick ??crick crick crick crick crick shashaSEXX
XXcrick crick crick
               ?crick crick XX   ?   %tsha   ? XX   ? crick
?sha   XX   ?crick Xcrick crick X   ?crick crick %shaX ?X   ?crick
crick   shacrick crick tcrick shashashacrick crick
       ?crick crick crick shaXX??crick tXX ?crick tXX??crick ?crick ? sha   crick
crick crick crick shaX   crick sha crick ?   X
    shaX   crick crick crick shaX   ?   ? tshashaScrick crick crick shaX   crick crick ?
tshashaX?SEX   crick crick
        crick X   ?crick crick sha XshaX ??   ?   SEX   crick ?crick
crick crick crick crick
        crick shaX ?   Xcrick crick crick crick crick crick shaXX   SEXX   crick crick
shacrick crick crick   Xsha XX   ? ?   crick
        crick crick crick   ?% shaX ?crick crick crick crick crick crick crick crick
shaX??crick crick crick X??   shashaX??crick crick XXcrick crick   ???crick crick crick

27

Start trying to break it out
    I started trying to break it down, to field-ground the gestalt out of the soundscape, and I thought
        break-it break-it break-it
        break-it break-it break-it
        break-it break-it break-it

and intense wave of psychadelic effect came over me,

as usual Blake had a wild gleam in his eye,
off in the distande I could see the patterns of waves

        ~~~~~~~~~~~~~~~~~~~~
        ~~~waves~~~~~~~~~~~~
        ~~~~~~~~~waves~~~~~~~
        ~~~~~~~~~~~~~~~~~~~~

you've got the one thing following another,
and you've got the layers coming in space.

/——/_____/===========/ ————/——————— _____/

    I started trying to break it down, to field-ground the gestalt out of the soundscape, and I thought

        bracket bracket break-it bracket bracket
        break-it bracket break-it break-it bracket
        bracket bra ket bracket bracket bra ket
        bra ket break-it bracket bra ket bra ket
        bracket bracket bracket bra ket bra ket
        bracket .... bra ket bra ket
        bracket .... bra ket bracket
        <a h a> bracket bracket bracket bracket
        bracket bracket bracket bracket bracket
        bracket bracket bracket bracket bracket
        bracket bracket bracket bracket bracket

Somehow this white noise, this union of of opposties would be the <u>silence</u> (phase cancelation) But there is always someting goin in and out of the time continuouum and I thought what if I tried to cleave space bracket

       bracket bracket bracket bracket bracket
       bracket bracket bracket bracket bracket
       bracket bracket bracket bracket bracket
       bracket bracket bracket bracket bracket
       bracket bracket bracket bracket bracket
       bracket .... bracket bracket
       bracket .... bracket bracket
       bracket bracket bracket bracket bracket
       bracket bracket bracket bracket bracket
       bracket bracket bracket bracket bracket
       bracket bracket bracket bracket bracket

                break-it   bracket   bra ket   <a a>   aha!!
    a matrix of <> goes in the spaces, perhaps,

bracket bracket bracket bracket bracket

       bracket <aHa> .... bracket
       bracket .... <aHa> .... bracket
       bracket .... <aHa> bracket
       bracket bracket bracket bracket bracket

       <a h a> <a H a> <a H a> <a H a> <a H a> <a H a>

of Dirac , where you bracket two phenomena together, the dual space, the space of all possible combinations a thing can be, and there is the envelope of probability out there.
    Layer of sound.
    I started thinking about Dirac,
    and how would he attack this problem, yes the Dirac attack

a potential entelechy

shaka shaka shaka attack the Dirac attack

yes the Dirac attack, a formal way of attacking any problem can be summed up in what is the bracket the bra and the ket <a|H|a>

this is what the <a|H|a>, the bra and the ket means

1. Get a vector space,
2. Span it with as many basis vectors as you need
3. Write the Hamiltonian for the energy of the space.
This Hamiltonian is a matrix of eigenvalues, or measurable frequencies that operates on the eigenvector of the system. The eigenvector is that combination of basis vectors which most symmetrically maps the observables to that space.

That is the bra and the ket <a|H|a>

from that principle can be derived most of the rest of quantum mechanics, *ab initio*, and it certainly is a general formulation of the problem for any space that is (symmetry) adaptable to the linear algebra of vector spaces. Including harmonic spaces (Hilbert Spaces)

anyway
it already seems like such a long time since I explored this stuff.
I think I'll write a paper on the Semiotics of Symbiosis

might be something called,
How Nature
Applies the Vector Space Formalism of Quantum Mechanics
to Create a Noo-Sphere for Semiotic Evolution
at a Molecular Biology Level,
or something like that.
Probably already been done, and if you know about it please let me know so I needn't bother.

So if we were to try and apply a semiotic
sign reading
approach to the situation with biology, in particular any symbiosis or coevolution

we could say that the symbiosis of two entities, <a and a> is such that the action H of the system would try to minimize the use of energy,
while of course producing entropy.

In other words you think of this dual space of ...

—I think: what if you described this philosophy the way Joe Bob describes a slasher film (Archibald Wheeler at UT. dispatching ideas).

Dirac
Wheeler
Prigogene
a kind of intellectual Cyrano de Bergerac wielding a semiotic rapier.

distraction, —
I started to look for the explanation of a dual space.
and wonder about how it might apply a communications and
entropy and a kind of code processing.
This is the demon part, the Maxwell daemon for the thought
experiment.

but then I get distracted by

Prigogene
Ilya Prigogene
gog
gene
engine
prick-o-gene
I'd see him at lectures with his accent he used to love to draw
out the word
fluctuations
fluke-to-ations
flook-chew-ashuns
and talked about stabilizations in non linear, far from equilibrium dynamical systems

anyway, back to the dual space
certainly most of quantum mechanics is based upon a communication model, certainly all the Bose particles, photons are
considered conveyers of information, an exchange particle, a
quanta of the field

the dual space came out of Heizenburg's uncertainty, the non
commutativity of momentum and position, with its deeper
implications about space and causality.

we are NOT in Euclidean Kansas anymore

Dirac introduces the bra and ket from the word bracket to
denote the use of parts of the bracket. The half brackets were
for state vectors and their eigenvalues

and the action was the operator or the photon of communication that extracted the eigenvalue from the eigenvector, that produces the observable.

I think about the first time I measured the charge
it was the Milican oil experiment,
in which you watched through a spyglass as a droplet of oil
moves through a potential field
you know the viscosity and the size the field moving the
droplet and its velocity and you compute the charge on the
electron.

but it was like watching bubbles rise in an amber beer,
only it was this kind of blue field,
and I am looking at it now as if the experiment were taking
place right in front of my eyes,
but it might be just phosphenes moving against the sky

the semiotics of symbiosis

semiotics
semi-augh-tics
auguring clock tick
boring into the future
auhg?!
awe

semi
cicadae
cuts clippers
lacunae
cuts across the body of consciousness

2 barriers:
relativistic velocities
uncertainty
both come together in Dirac
discrete energy quanta, implies digital algebra
matrices
matrices and operators also were the formalism for the curved spaces
we were very privileged to study that in undergraduate school

dual space of light
on the one hand it was like a wave
on the other like a particle
light as a particle with momentum, a vector
light as a wave with colored radiation

the dual space
it answers the question, what other dimension can I find to
project this argument such that this a pace will most succinctly
display the observable attributes of the situation.

onto / slashology

```
         /      \ __\      __/    __
    -/-  __   /    \/  /  /     /    \
     /    /        \__    //_        \
    /              \    /  __         |
    |        __     \/+-/            /
     \__       \     \              /
       \__            |            /
        \   /___      / /      |  /  \
         ___/    __      \/  /\     )
          \__    /      /    |   |  /'
          /  \___/  \        /   //
     // / / // / /\     /-_-/\//-__-
     /  /  // /  \__// / / /   //
        p/q   \___/   \        /
     / / / /\    /-_-/\-__-
    / S/Z  /  \__ / / /
intuitive/spiritual   imaginative/heuristic  /
left/right  /
    /  /id/ego/   [q,p]/[p,q]/
   /  conscious/unconscious        /
              /   / /
   / / / / /persona/mask/      /
  / / / /     /
   /   /   /   / / / /
aesthetic/meaning/            /  / /
   / / / / /conceptual/concrete/    /
analog/digital   / /diachronic/synchronic/
    /form/feeling    /    /I/eye/ /
 / /    / /  / / / /
   /  /      / / /
   /mystirium conjunctionem/naugual  /  /
```

         and I am (listening)there
                        ))) listening (((
                  (0) (o)   (o)))))o(((((

         (. .. " .. :.   <<'~~~!!)o(!>!'
         !))o((!::. ~~!:('   '... '~~!:!:(:
            '~!!<::. `'.-)))o(((.``):. `~!!!:
         !!!('!:::... '!!!!: ~~~   ":. '
         !<!!!!h.)!!!::.'!<!)))o(((:.~!~ ~ ~~>'

                 /   \./   \/_   /\   /\   /\/\/\/\/\/\/\.-.-.-
            __{!_ _eⁱ_   )   eⁱ/!\   / \ / \ /
           /   /_/!\._eⁱ_/   //   /___/   \/   \/
          ((__{(@)eⁱ__eⁱ.//_/__   ____----
           __/{/(_)_eⁱ   )\\ \\-   ____---
              ((__)_)_/   )\ \>--------------------
               __/   __/\/\/
                  __,--'

Peyote sings through the archetypes of perception to jumpstart seeing

Think of Something Big — Nature at Play

nature at play

energy build up in the distortion field
caught in a temporal loop
decision omission
a highly localized distortion of the space time continuum

try to think about an entity
a force much bigger than a planet
a force that plays,
eucaryote
you carry it
a you chariot
octave scale wheel of 5ths | 12, scale not universal
                           octave the e^{ijwt}th is the same
sound over
                           it is the ruler
                           the metric in music space
resting consonances, parsing distances
s/+ 1/2 nd harmonic you hear one.
We are hard wired for octaves
overtones are related. Psychoacoustic beats
consonance a major is a third is "pretty"
                           psychoacoustic tends to be heard
                           the same note. Different way
                           of breaking up the interval
visualize rhythm
all art including music aspires to the level of nature at play

surrealism blows away boundaries

it is about impedance matching,

the idea is to get your nervous system to
recognized that you have artificially constructed boundaries
to what's really out there.

The Vedic system is about tuning
tuning, all kinds of tuning,
diatonic, equi-tempered, ...
kinds of tuning in which the distances between events and
things are seen as a proportional and not linear distance from
other things,
a evil tyrant is a 3rd "harmonic" away
from a good man

we made this distinction called body and another called mind,
and we take drugs in a kind of
synchromesh, stichomythia, sick-o-mythia
stinko-machia
to be able to shift gears into the higher harmonics and receive
the universe without a whole lot of artificial logical and other
distinction and the impediments of
impedance mismatch
getting in the way,
hook the cable directly to the signal,
and go through the tunnel opened up

we made the distinction between the river and it's bank and we

can take down that distinction,
the river can be the wind carrying notes of leaves in a skittering
scuttling song
and some notes can be propositions

or it could be the river is this pampas, and I am running
through it and the notes are time animals, going up and down
scales

peyoteros must change the names of things

When you eat peyote you should take a walk
in Nature.
Nature walks are important
They're important because peyoteros need to understand the
world of our surroundings.
We need to learn the REAL names of things
The trees. The mountains. The lakes. The birds.
peyoteros do that by changing the names of things

I like to call our sun (N*)

(N*) is a star of many brothers in the galaxy,
He is a single star, the father, a loner.
The father was degenerate, not like the others, caught up in the
old ways, locked in a binary dance around another.
He broke away went solo
or just hung out with other loose degenerates
who couldn't reach binary stardom.
Traveled away lived apart,
got his own crew to run with
in the great milky spew

N* is the Father
n$^{@°}$ is the Mother

n$^{@°}$ represents the planet in the life zone,
where life starts.
It has to have moons around it,

It has to have a family, a big uncle like Jupiter
that can protect the young $n^{@°}$ from constant bombardment
during the accretion period.
$n^{@°}$ has her own moon,
like a mirror,
that pulls on her tides.
Did I mention how the lovely $n^{@°}$ was awash in the ebb and
flow of inundation and desiccation.

But I'm getting ahead of myself
but what would be the real name of water

Mother $n^{@°}$ that we call Gaia
Mother $n^{@°}$ and Father $N*$
—Father and Mother together $N*n^{@°}$

they had an eldest daughter that we call ne^{lo}
and the oldest daughter ne^{lo} goes ne_{lo} down into the planet
ne_{lo} is the probability that life originate if conditions are
suitable, ne_{lo} goes ne^{lo} down into the planet and she imbues
the planet aggrandizes out and becomes ne^{lo} exponentiating
out first into some early phases water whose real name is H_2O
whose real name is

$$\omega\Pi\int ter(\wp)$$
and wind whose real name is
$$\omega\Pi(i,n,d(e^{in})/dt)$$
and fire $f(\int eire\ )$

The name of the wind

I got into trying to visualize phase space.
looked for attractors,
like dust devils and other self-perpetuating turbulent forms
—
I had long enjoyed going out into storms,
we were after all in tornado alley.

I tried to visualized the phase space of the atmosphere,
tried to see in the sky the behavior of rising thermal currents,
in the heat shimmers.

atmosphere at rest;
atmosphere in ordered convection;
atmosphere in turbulent convection;

Chaos attractors were something I thought I could see
in the shimmers of the heat rising off things.
What were they due to,
van Gogh painted them over and over in his paintings,

I now had a name for the wind.
and I called it

$$\omega \Pi(i,n,d(e^{in})/dt)$$

$\omega \Pi(i, n, d(e^{in})/dt)$

where

ω is for angular velocity
Π is the permutation operator looks at all the possibilities of ways the wind can go
i,   is an index of the element in a vector (dimension)
n,   is the Reynolds number, designating the medium
$d(e^{in})/dt$
    is the velocity of the exponential expansion flow in time on the complex plane

The wind was actually an invisible fractal dendrite,
unfolding in the time dimension
that you could see when it flowed through and bumped into
things at its boundary; it reached out and touched as many
things as it could. It was a representation in real visual space of
attractor activity in a phase space of many dimensions:
how strong the wind was,
the temperature difference between the up and downdraft
currents
and the mirror term:(Π , the permutation operator)
in which the wind/attractor sensed its own motion at its boundaries, and in a kind of feedback adjusted accordingly
Whew!
This stuff gets you wild in your mind don't it?

```
                    /   \./   \/\_
               __{!\_  _ei_    )   eⁱ  /!\
            /   /\_/!\._eⁱ  _/   //   /
           (   (__{(@)eⁱ \__ei.//_/__
           \__/{/(_)\_eⁱ    )\\ \\-
              (    (__)_)_/   )\ \>
               \__/       \__/\/\/
                   \__,-'
```

What would René say

I had made it out to the patch and was sitting sweating under the old mesquite tree. The mesquite tree's leaves are so waxy and durable it makes them looks so paleo hanging down like a weeping willow.

"I understand you dabble in metaphysics."

I found myself repeating that line from a cartoon. The cartoon has one guy with his leg dispersing into a tree; another guy, trying to remain cool, is saying "I understand you dabble in metaphysics," to him.

I noticed the transparent casing of a cicada, its outer body left still clinging to the underside of a tree branch. Dead philosophers. Metaphysics. I think of my old friend Jules Windish. He is the only person I knew who could conceivable be called a metaphysician. I went and got him and brought him to the land for a day in the country.

Jules Windish. My old mentor, bearded, skinny, flailing his arms like windmills when he walked, wild and intense, (he was such a quixotic figure). My philosopher friend looked a lot like a younger, more intense Ezra Pound. And his name, I never knew if it was Jewels or Joules, you couldn't buy a better name.

I had found him, sure enough, where I thought he'd be, on campus freeloading in the Philosophy library. I told him it was good for philosopher's to get a day in the country. I wanted him to see the patch (he loved marijuana, said it was *the* Philosopher's Stone).

He thought he was some kind of Socrates at the campus and he was. We had been roommates and occasionally did psychedelics together and talked for hours and hours. I tried to keep up with him. He would launch into some explication of a Plato dialog while walking in the park. It was hilarious in the morning when we jumped onto a shuttle bus into campus and he'd be full of vigor just as likely to start up a one-sided conversation with a groggy student, —a complete stranger — about Heidegar! Life for him was an endless philosophical fight between he as defender and lover of wisdom and the sophists. He'd even use their methods to tease them. Like he'd spy a pretty girl with glasses, get into her face and launch into a syllogism:

"Brains wear glasses;"

"Scientist are brains."

"Therefore, you must be a scientist."

Then he'd launch into some harangue and frighten her.

One time we went to a Psychic Faire. In those early days, a Psychic Faire was generally a happy affair, booths, tables, seekers milling. You had all these new age types with their crystals, and tarot and aroma therapy and neo-Reichian body work. It was all quite new, breakthrough stuff, and people were vulnerable and excited to be espousing this new hope-filled insight into the world. Joules spent the whole time sidling along with his back to the walls of the room, sometimes even moving through the back of a booth this way, and he'd say, "I'm a mathematical philosopher." He was definitely outstandingly weird even in this crowd, and he was completely without social grace, unable to understand the copious amounts of paranoia he induced in these people with his antics.

He always wore a light-colored, striped, and very rumpled seersucker suite that he must have got out of a freebox. In the Texas heat he looked like some down and out fallen southerner refugee from the Raj in India, one of those unshaven sweaty ne'er-do-wells hanging around the Casaba, shady and down on his luck in his tie and button down collar. He was an original: a 60s blue scholar worker with a battered leather satchel full of these marvelous logical koans. He would swing it back and forth by its leather strap and whenever he saw me he would open it up and hand me, a page of ultra-terse, hyperpithy writing which started out with a couple of clear statements, them moved into logical equations written out in the symbolic notation of Russell and Whitehead.

He'd shake his head in dismay, indicate the *hoi paloi* and say, "All they want is tarot and astrology."

"What would Rene say?" That was his favorite all purpose quote.

"What would Rene say, " he'd start in a mock exasperated way and launch into his kind of nagging monologue.

"Logical analysis is the only way to interpret reality!" he'd offer.

And I'd take him up on it, "No way, Rene! "What about feelings," I'd quote that Youngblood song: 'You can feel what you need to know'. That would usually set him off pretty good.

Except Joules, wasn't joking, he really did try to be like

some kind of Descartes/Spock hybrid.

He'd come back blustery, emphatic, with "It is necessary to suspend all interpretation of experience that are not absolutely certain."

It was wonderfully incongruous, "Rene, man," I'd say to him, "you've got to expand your horizons."

We had worked on a book together called the Diamond Cutter's Sutra. It was about Russell and Whitehead, and it had all these amazing koan-like semantic resonators reverberating in logical space. They were real head trips. It was our own Varieties of Logical Experience (based on Varieties of Religious Experience and Varieties of Psychedelic Experience) crossed with *the* Diamond Sutra. I had an essay in it —the Poem as Mandala —which was about the Jungian interpretation of literature. That book is lost.

I never knew whether he was putting me on or what, but he was a real philosopher. I wrote a whole memoir of our experiences hanging out and bumming around Austin, called Ontological Hysteria and the Austintacious stomp. It was written during the Cosmic Cowboy craze in Austin. As far as I know it is still stashed in my sister's attic in San Antonio. Don't suppose that book will every see the light of day.

As I was sitting there contemplating the transparent carcass of a cicada, I recalled his visit out to the patch.

When finally we got out to the land, after many misadventures, —I had to pick him up in Ruth's car, I took him out to the patch because he was completely honest and without guile.

And sure enough, —we were out there underneath the mesquite tree, he'd leaned back casual against the tree—he looked at me in an older-brother, monastic way and said, "You know, Walker, we must make a good accounting of ourselves out here."

"Why's that?"

"We're philosophers aren't we? And we must do what philosophers do."

"And what's that."

"There was something about it in Phaedrus..."

"Plato's dialog?"

"Yes. It is a dialog about the immortality of the soul... Yes, now let me think what was that dialog about? Let me recall now, —winged souls in the Phaedrus."

"Winged souls?" I said. "Wow those old philosophers were a pretty raucous bunch weren't they. They really used to get spaced out."

Windish gave me a slightly pained look and said, "Yea spaced out on philosophy."

"Winged souls and the cicada-men," Joules kept thinking aloud. "Oh yes now I recall. Yea... It is in a beautiful scene: Socrates is telling Phaedrus... that they must conduct themselves with grace else the cicadas will report back to the muses. They are kicking back under a tree and Socrates says, that they must be good philosophers and seek wisdom or else the cicadas will report back to the muses that they were not.

Socrates tells him : "otherwise the cicadas would be laughing at us and thinking we are just a couple of slaves who have escaped work and are going to sleep the afternoon away under a tree. No, we must be talking and conversing and actively seeking truth and beauty so that they will not report ill of us back to the muses." Or something like that.

It's cool the way Plato has these looping reaching-out moments in his dialogs that, though they seem to be tangential asides, are actually moments where Plato goes out of the sticky logical argument, to bring in some aesthetic phenomena from another dimensions like myth, to drive home his point. But it is also something real, that looks like it could happen.

His dialogs mirror the penetrating way the mind has of dancing around some new phenomena, the way the mind thinks, the way it settles down to throw a gestalt around some phenomena. Consciousness is a strange attractor. Have you heard of that, chaos theory, and that. And you know, in our time, theories perform the same function as myth. They are like heuristic footholds which the mind can struggle and climb up to understanding.

Socrates tells Phaedrus a myth about how the cicadas came about. He tells him that the old people believed that the cicadas were originally men. That the muses had turned these men on to Music. The men were so enthralled by Music that they could not stop singing. They began chanting and singing all the live long day until they wasted away to nothing. Apparently the muses felt guilty and let the men become these little disembodied winged creatures that lived on and on forever. They didn't need food or drink. They sang all the time. And ever since then, these cicadas keep a watch on the world and report back to the muse.... Yea, that was a cool dialog.

I got this picture of me having to sit down and die in the forest . I'm just sitting in the sun, unable to move, life sucked out of me like a cicada that has shed its body, just a clear shell of a thing just sitting there life sucked out of me looking at the green scene. Got this picture of me going golden.

Me: "Ah yea, now I remember," though I couldn't remember it that well.

Jules: " Plato seems to be describing the souls of men, —as they fly —as these little disembodied entities that fly around and can get into other people.

"And Socrates is talking about the immortality of the soul, he describes how the body looses its soul in terms of the cicadas metamorphosing out of their skin!"

Me: "It was about rhetoric wasn't it? Yea it's cool."

minute by minute I am melting, my skin is melting off,

the fluids in it draining out slowly,

leaving a transparent shell of a man

the heat is astounding,

stupefying

it takes your breath away.

Jules: "Oh yea... It ends beautifully, he talks about how the philosophers, the lovers of wisdom, will be at the end of their days. Yes that's right, he talks about the cicadas as being like the souls of men having to go through this rebirth process.

Me: "I didn't know the Greeks had rebirth, that was just a thing for Buddhist and eastern philosophy."

Jules: "Well back then all the philosophers all over the

world were mystical. They still are. Socrates just wanted everybody to be philosophers and lead the well-ordered life.

Jules: "He likened the process of being a philosopher to cicadas trying to get their wings: people who did not lead a well ordered life had to go back into the darkness, under the earth, after death in order to come back up and get their wings, while philosophers who had led a well ordered life, got their wings at death, and could come out and fly around.

Me: "Wow, that sounds a lot like the Tibetan book of the dead."

Jules: "Exactly."

Me: "For Plato, then the Cicada was a model for the human soul.

Jules: "Yea, it is curiously like the way the cicada gets out of its shell. Plato went into gross detail about how this moisture, this kind of ectoplasm, they called phlogiston flows out of the eyes, flows over his body, moistens the buds of his wings, softens the hard parts of the etheric body that confined the wings and prevented them from growing before, so that now the stalks of the wings grow from their roots until they cover the whole form of the soul. He describes the process like the cutting of teeth.

Me: "Wow, that sounds pretty terrifying," I said. "Like it would be a cool horror movie. Some kind of philosophical slasher flick, like when the werewolves undergo metamorphosis?"

Jules: "Jesus! Why can't you ever be serious. You're really annoying. You've got some kind of hard-headed defense against learning? Those guys were really something. They really believed the soul motivated the body. We've lost that vision."

"I mean the whole idea of the heaven and hell thing was around way before the Church, The Church got this idea that they could make a self sustaining community out of people who feared death, —and who doesn't — by mapping out a plan for the afterlife. All religions do this. But the Church is areally conservative force. It dumbs down spirituality.

"Yet there are some beautiful divine contemplation's and art and music coming out of the Church."

I knew that Jules enjoyed going to Church very much.

" Anyway," he continued, "the ancient people looked at the natural processes and through them saw how the soul, as the animating thing that moved people around, escaped from the body at death, and flowed around through all things.

He had gotten me kind of embarrassed. Still I didn't back down. " Is the soul a massless particle, a boson," I teased. "Could it pass through a mountain like a neutrino,"

"Easy, " he said not taking up the bait.

"And it in the underground realm between death and rebirth," he continued, shifting into a high oratory mode, preaching "the soul which has lost its wings, is carried along until it settles on something. Until it is subsumed in a terrestrial body."

Jules continued: "Be not deceived. Even though the body looks like it can move under its own power, it is the soul that animates it, the immortal soul.

Me: And the soul of philosophers take wing at death and they are not reborn. Like a Bodhisatva?"

Jules "Right, they are philosophers that choose not to leave but come back and help out. I'm a Bodhisatva."

I got this image of Bodhisatva Windish as this angular flat-dimensional kind of cartoon guy standing next to a tree. Part of him is turning into this transparent shell there.

He is purposely taking a step and passes his left foot through the tree. His left foot looks to be dissolved into the tree, He is looking over at me with his flat 2 dimensional face in a kind of leer.

I wipe the sweat off my brow from the rushy hallucinations, the moisture pouring out of my eyes at the impossibility of this drug induced figment of my imagination but my mind doesn't know the difference and even though the hair is standing up on my head and I'm scared speechless I'm so stoned I walk toward him and say "I understand you dabble in metaphysics."

"Why yes as a mater of fact I do," he says. "How did you know."

"Well I see the way you foot is half dispersed into the tree.' I say, mater of factly.

"What do you make of that?" he says.

"Well," I say, "I thought you might be a manifestation of partial spatio/temporal concrescence."

"Right you are," he says with a wink.

God that really cinches it, I think. I'm out here wandering around not only having hallucinations but talking to them.

I wanted a language with which I could "stand aside from" or "get into" things but this is way over the edge.

"Hmm," he says, "have you tried induction."

He slowly faded out of sight, the last thing to go being his Cheshire cat put-on style smile.

Even so the smiling mouth continued its lecture. "So you see this underground is like hell, where the soul has to be corrected, and from which it emerges (just as the wingless cicada does), free itself from its mortal and inert body (just as the cicada emerges from its integument), and grow its wings again."

And Windish continues in the air, "Plato goes on in the Phaedrus to get this whole visionary thing going about the gods making their way, along with the soul of the philosopher, poking through the vault of heaven to look at the star-maker machinery and how it is like, the cicada emerging from beneath the surface of the earth onto another plane of experience on which it is transformed from a wingless to a winged state.

"Yea it's a real fine dialog."

The Tree of Life

I lay down against the trunk of a tree,
relaxing back against some big roots
which formed a kind of chair,
as they went into the ground there,
to have a good think.
I looked up
through the branches
at patches of blue sky coming through
the spaces
and I saw the clouds,
as dendritic fingers
and the branches in the tree as dendritic fingers too.
Yess, that's the fractal signature
zigzaggy fingers snaking out from
one domain into another:
Is Mother Nature a Strange Attractor?
I can remember the day that I began to flip
into a new paradigm of nature.
      It was in the evening time,
just at that crossover time
when the day gives way to night
and the moon was already up,
a perfect white circle in the blue sky.
And I saw the clouds,
as fingers snaking out
reaching, as if the moon

was some anachronistic throwback of platonic form
in the hip new modern Mandelbrot set,
which was trying to cling to its past.
And it was like the moon was a circular dynamo
or the generator
against which all the world
was bending and dancing,

I had been looking into chaos and fractals and cellular automata that was just starting to come in then. We were just starting to read some of the literature in the journals from hippie physicists in Santa Cruz, and from a supreme uptown geometer in the service of his employer at IBM, Dr. Mandelbrot..

And that day I couldn't look at anything
without seeing fractals
    I'd look at a branch
    see it reaching up it's twig-tips
    so symmetrical
    branching
one domain into another.
And I saw how the clouds though different,
    --soft at the edges,
    not clearly demarcated like the branches
—due to non-linearities,
    no doubt were fractals too.
That's the interesting part

what goes on
at the boundaries,
—little winds,
      turbulent curlicues
make it all so soft & diffuse.
Yes it was the dendrites!
From that day on I saw fractals everywhere.
In the frieze of trees, with their gnarly branches
or pouring milk into my coffee
and in high satellite pictures of the world,
its deltas,
    its marshes,
        zooms of the way the sea and the land interact
of course coastlines-the classical fractal.
Or taking a piss, I'd watch the bubbles cloning out around the singularity of the stream, watching the dendrites between the bubbles there, going out as shockwaves bouncing off the boundaries of the bowl as wave behavior passing out to the boundary of the bowl, the bubbles mounting, reflecting.
The bubbles were like little
cellular automata tiling the plane,
like grass dropping seeds, which lay dormant;
then when conditions are right
    spring into life,
as if some kind of automaton were sampling
what's going on all around it
and making decisions based on that —
a world of rules, simple rules.

Then a big black bird swoops
down and squabbles with a smaller bird over
some leavings.
    —contention of 2 species
dynamic system seeking equilibrium.

In the geometry of chaos I was starting to recognize
a beautiful flowing wholeness
all around us.
I began to be able to feel it.
In smoke rising from a cigarette, I can smell it.
Something was turned on like a faucet
going from laminar flow to forceful blast.

Like the distributed fractal of the immune system
of which She is no doubt most proud,
Mother Nature is a strange attractor and she is all around us
flowing within and without you.

Is mother nature a strange attractor?
I don't mean in the sense of attracting strangeness,
the strange attractor
does not attract strangeness,
I mean in the sense of Nature...
—Evolution — is a process by which the more manageable
chaos is attracted out of randomness, out of noise.
It is a kind of tuning, in the sense of wanting to extract some

kind of entity, pattern or shape that continues to perpetuate itself.

I got myself as comfortable as I could laying at the base of the tree. I shut my eyes for a moment, then opened them slowly and just let them drift, ...drift up along the branches. I let my mind float on the breeze over the boughs, and out to where there were leaves on the trees.
I watched its movement,
as it danced and played
with
 the wind and the light.

What is it? that tells the tree
to branch here,
and not there.

I thought of ole Ez's poem about becoming a tree:
"I became a tree amid the wood,"
something, something,
"and many things became clear to me,
that were rank folly to my head before."
And then I let my mind diffuse and it went into the tree. Now here I have to say, that it is beyond my most poetical abilities as a writer to translate into words what it was like to move through the branching tree boughs as if I had been sucked down by a living thing, a hydra of hollowed out tunnels fanning out, from — and into — the limitless green bank fractal at the heart of the world. It was like being

inside a tree machine, Phylum and phloem these regular perfect cellular automata for moving water and energy. Mystics and thinkers have used the Indian Mandala, the Celtic Knot, Yagsadrill, Setheroth, the multifoliate rose, the Bo tree, The tree in the Garden of Eden, and other shapes, to symbolize and conceptualize the swimming rush of falling headlong into the far-from-equilibrium collection of attractors that is Mother Nature. Other modern symbols for this great multidimensional energy distribution system have been given to us by: Mandelbrot, who used fabulous iterated color fractals to show the turbulent flow and iterated structure of this chaotic geometry; Prigogene who used the far-from-equilibrium dissipative structures of thermodynamics; Eiger who used the autocatalytic hypercycle; and von Neuman the cellular automata. I recall these modern models in the same breath as the ancient analogies because they bear for me the same relationship to the tree of life: they are cross sections of the flow. The ecology of earth has a fractal microstructure, that is to say it is a folding over, a scaling of levels of self-similar microcosms in the macrocosm. The ecology of earth is an attractor of attractors, it is a cycle of hypercycles and it is a swarm of cellular automata in parallel and it is a statistical ensemble of dissipative structures on a par with nothing else that we know about yet in the universe.

But what I shall now write down will be serial, because language is serial. It is programmed into my memory, and I'll try to output what I saw.

Looking up the trunk of the tree, I saw a structure uniting heaven and earth, I saw it as a slow explosion, mushrooming up into the clouds, and felt its fingers digging deep down into the earth, white root fingers eating earth, eating earth.
This is what I saw: the spheres of influence.
Spheres within sphere, with the sun at the center, then the clear blue sphere of the atmosphere around it, then the hydrosphere, around that, then the sphere of green plants that can convert sunlight to food enclosing that, and the sphere of the herbivores and on top of that the thin sphere of the omnivores. Then going all around that the even thinner shell of society, a nervous interconnected network of signs.
The earth enclosing the sun.
Then I see tunnels moving in and among all the spheres, tunnels opening up trying always to get the energy density flux to be as high as possible.

Beam me up Scotty!

Tunnels opening up
being picked up and pulled along as part of the flow
we are lifting off the earth in a kind of swarm

it is like you are zooming down a star field, these little dots getting larger as they come at you and some of them turning into icons and avatars, and you are zooming along with it, it is a semiotics of swarm,

tesseracts, a whole bunch of tesseracts,
and they are each themselves of flipping their space/time
panels looking out on each other, and at every corner
the cubes of 3 space
are pushing out to 4.

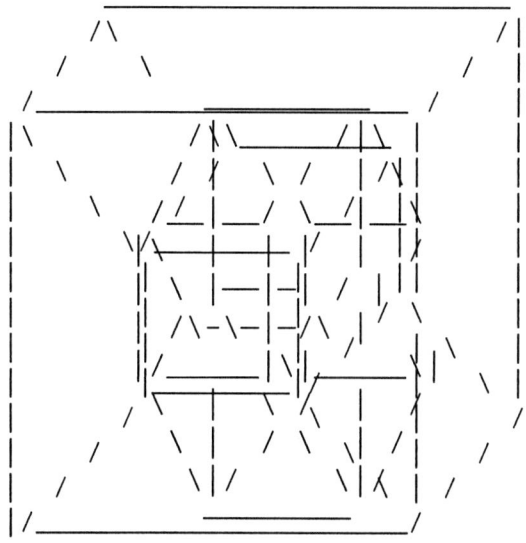

How we take to each other and get along,
how we try to further symbiosis,
even though at the local level we were in fierce competition.
We are expanding and contracting,
        throbbing
                in phase locked flow
and we are tumbling toward some kind of...we are attracted
around something, some kind of attractor is vaguely moving us
through space.
Like some kind of particles that had been scattered,
these people,

all these beings in the swarm
are moving toward some great end.
Like the rose of heaven
in the Dore illustrations of Dante's Paradiso,
like those rings around Saturn,
they are bodies that have gotten into a stable place
many great distances down the bifurcation diagram
of the dissipative structure.
The phase locked orbital rings create a bumping landscape,
that I realize is made from synthesized Fourier waves .
The wave picture easily merges with the surface picture when I
think of it as a hot body, a matrix of radiators that go in and out
and is transposed by a topology which lets it be one way or
another. The topology of the manifold!
Beam me up Scotty!
And there are fractals.
I can abstract fractals out of the flow,
We are all in a swarm, practicing the semiotics of swarm,
which is to move along with the flow
and not agitate too much on your neighbor,
and I think but wouldn't you like, for once, just for once,
to go across the current,
to move into your other stable orbit.

This is the green bank:
the various ways that Gaia stanches, stores and otherwise holds
back and uses the flow.
Flow is the real name of water

whose real name is
$\omega \Pi \int te^{r(\wp)}$
where
ω is the angular momentum of water, say in a vortex, and
Π is the permutation operator looks at all the possibilities of ways the water can go
and
$\int$ is the swath integral, integrating things over
t time
and
e is the base for expressing a wave like phenomena
and
r a function like the Reynolds number which expresses the level of control of the fluid in this medium, and that control is based on
$\wp$ a measure of potential to control or a fractal dimension

flow is

influenced by viscosity and density gradients

the ultimate viscosity or density is a boundary /

we speak of the direction of the flow:

stream wise;

and across the direction of flow:

span wise;

the synchronic and the diachronic

the boundary, the wall, the buffer zone,

lots of activity of the boundary, like questions of identity,

and port hole sense for that to pass through

I saw food flowing through an animal
diffusion across a wall
using chemical reaction
to change the wall viscosity gradient
I saw the first nervous systems of the hyrda,
capturing food in it's tentacles
I saw budding,
I saw gills for extracting oxygen from the water
I saw blastopores for extracting photons from the sun

over and over again the homology up and down the scale

I saw molecular trees connecting
and I saw morphological trees
branching into different evolutionary paths.

```
\ | /    *
 \ | * / *
 * | |   |
  | ` | /
   \ |
```

It was enough to make you want to get on your knees and
moan Stop, Stop. Stop!
Enough already!
These chemical transport and exchange are themselves cycles,
limit cycles
a kind of chaos extracted from the noise
differentiating itself out
as if to say, I am what I am.
A particular life form is a control strategy
whose morphology is based on the kind of environment
whence it emerges flow and the control goal to be achieved.

It is like the meshing of mechanical gears transferring energy,
but in this case it is hyper cycles, mainly of ATP spinning and
engaging enzymes which spin and output and engage other
enzymes, like a transmission. The cycles are like gears in a
transmission.
Control goals
for such flows include
transition delay/advancement,
mixing enhancement and noise suppression.
Not noise in the audial sense,
but noise in the sense of disturbing the signal
the signal, oh my god the signal.
Lets evolve language
and facial expressions to enhance the signal.
I let my mind float out into the field,
where a beast named hippocampus was getting excited
— and starting to shake in disbelief.
I could feel it there
        waiting,
                looking,
pqwing the ground
        agitated,
                wanting to run wild in the fields,
not caring to be ridden,
wanting to charge along the surf
        at the edge of things

```
                              _  __,;;;/
                           ,;( )_, )~\|
                           ;; //   `--.
                           '  \\    | '
```

Peyote

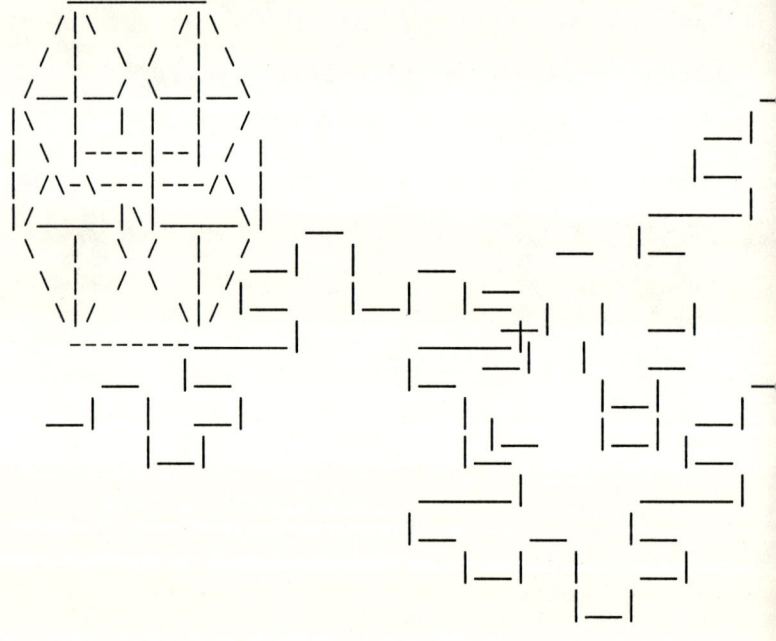

sings

Peyote

sings

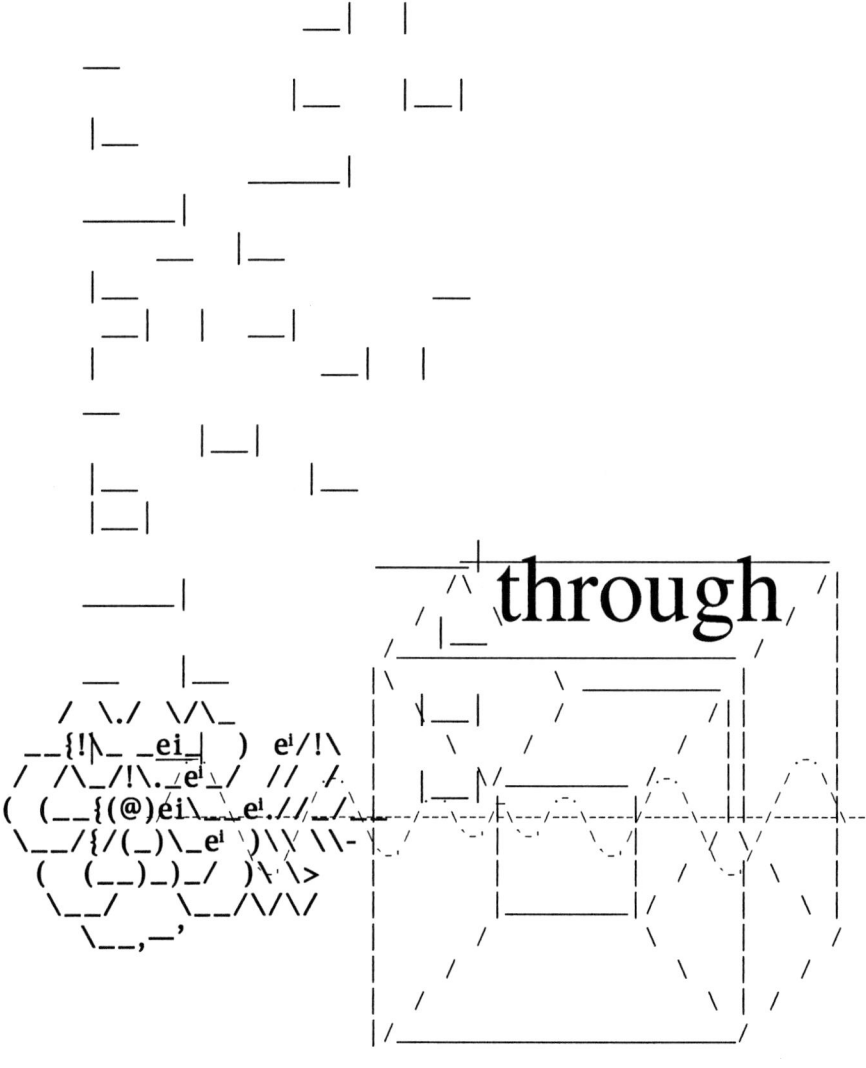

Peyote sings through

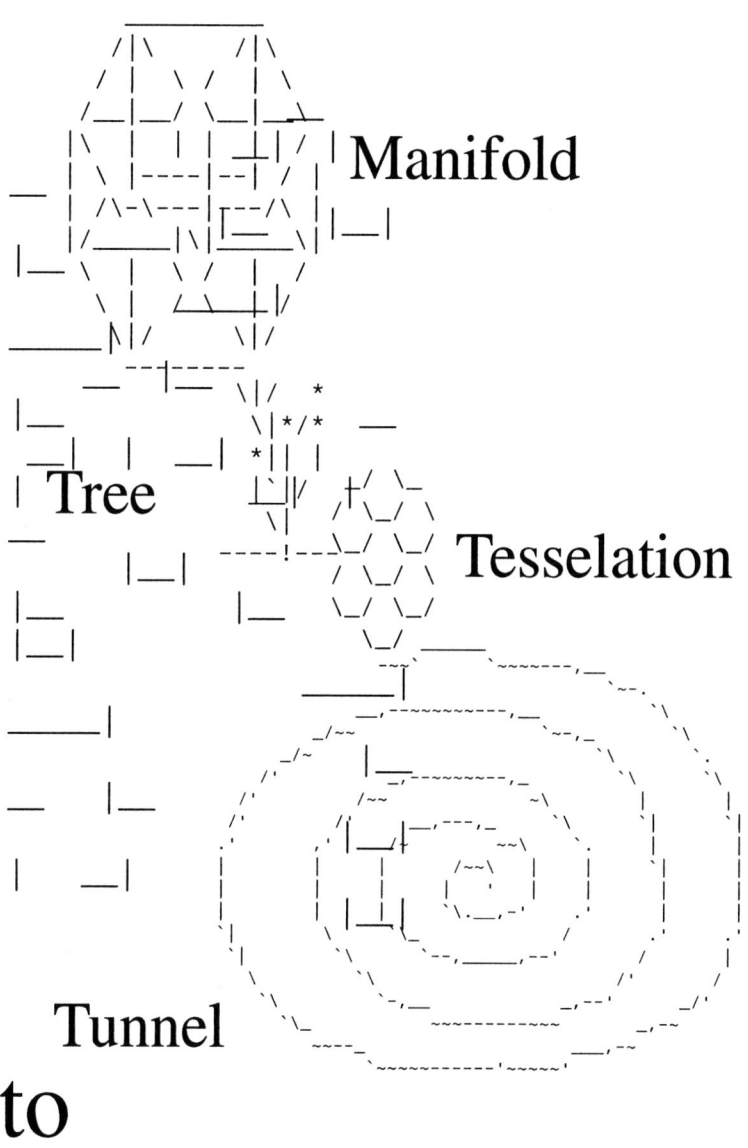

Manifold

Tree

Tesselation

Tunnel

to

jump-start

Seeing

Peyote sings through

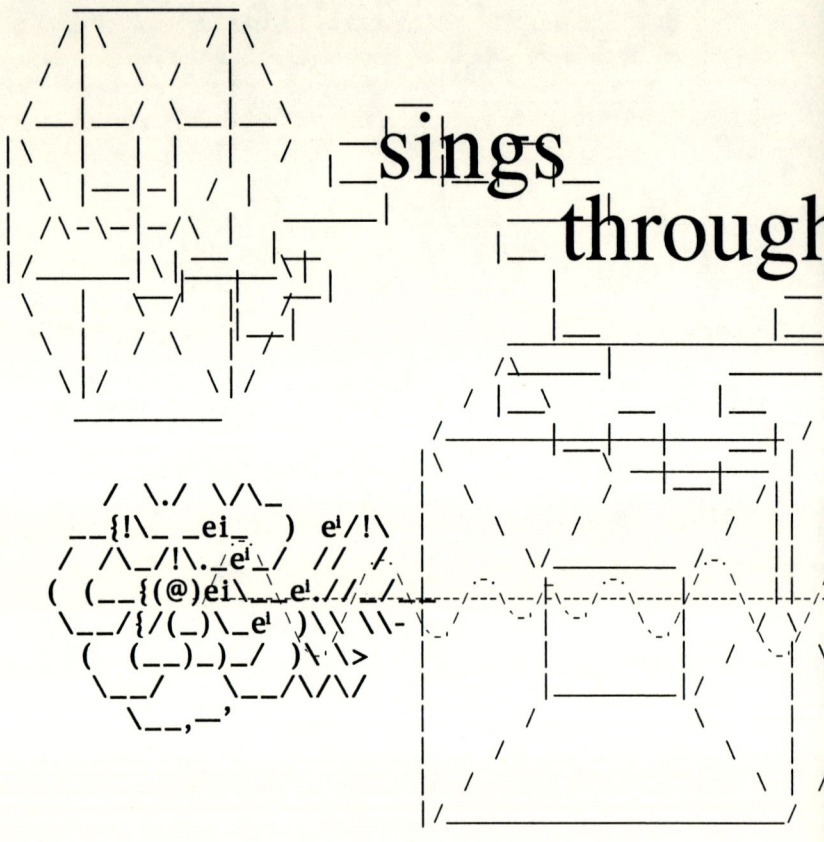

the archetypes of perception

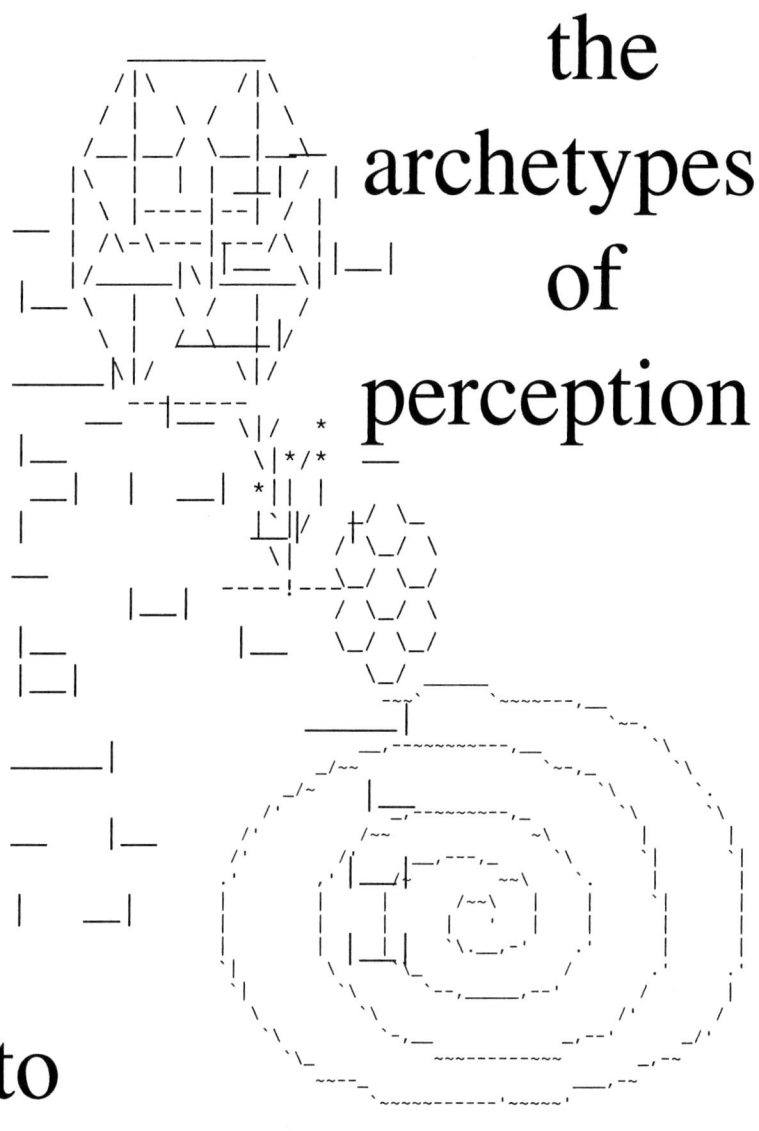

to jump-start Seeing

hyperspectral

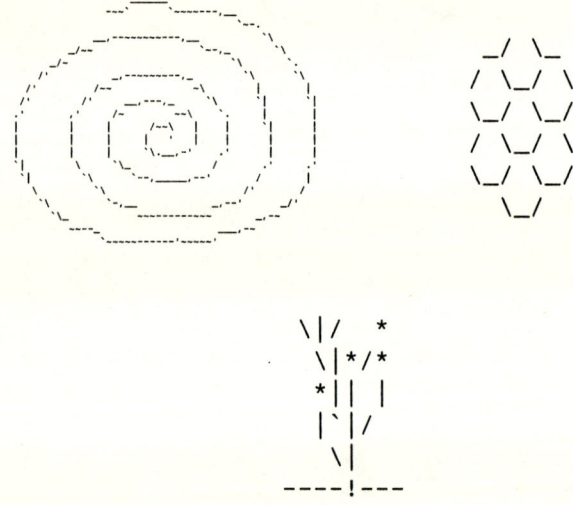

The Secret of the Cicadas's Song

part 2

Gaia and the Green Bank

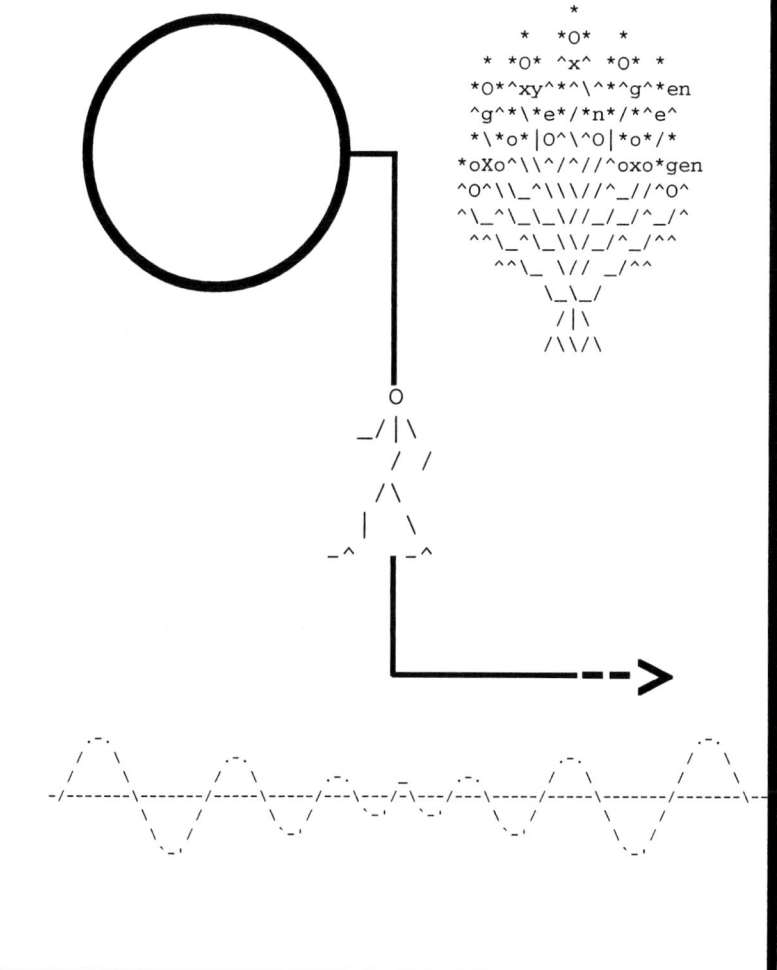

I too seem to be a fractal in the Green Bank

the green bank is an infinitely dimensional space, through with
fractals percolate in the odd dimension

I am my own theatre,
the theatre in which I dwell,
in the body which I must not sell.

Enter my ancestors,
father a boxer, hockey player
quick with figures, a dancer, a big man but very fast
run the table in pool halls, fight with a stick
alcoholic
never opened a book
married a beautiful country girl
petite, lolling against the door of an old ford
in shorts and a tight sweater,
a naive beauty, liked to jitterbug in the kitchen.
In years to come casting her eyes
heavenward, trapped.

and now I, young boho
from Austin and Berkeley
an older brother
an eccentric uncle
a scholar and a student of psychedelics.

relativity

got this picture
of the guy having to sit down and die in the forest

sitting out in the sun, life sucked out of him
like a cicada that has shed its body,
just a clear shell
       of a thing
just sitting there life sucked out of him
looking at the green scene
speculate on that! Mr. Out-of-Work Physicist!
"well it would have to get into
quantum mechanics
particle physics
information theory
uncertainty
Einstein's mass-energy relationship
acceleration as a second derivative
antimatter
the anthropic principle
the atmosphere
the big bang
kalpas
black holes
binding energy of atoms and
causality
cosmology
curved space
dimensions

energy
entropy
event horizon
evolution
field

gravity
Heizenberg uncertainty
impulse
life
light
matter
negative
organic matter
oxygen
parallel universes
vacuum
virtual
warp and
wormholes
and the human soul
to name a few of the topics."

an internal spirit
    I had as a child
        that i heard,
           that I have forgotten

to remake the spirit of harmony
to make the harmony
to search for this world

> it is up to the father to
> search for the strength
> to confront the old ghosts

we used to live in tribes,
in communes
we were so much a part
of the fabric of our world
that we got lost when we were away from it,
out of it,
had distanced ourselves from it

that is the thing that modern man
must feel, is how
terribly alone they are

Homo abstractus
has given up that sense of belonging
for a restless search
so that he may come
to know the universe
> stocking the illusive anti-proton

stocking the illusive anti-proton so that he can build an anti-matter warp engine and head of to the stars,

I have to say I'm kind of embarrassed
trying to take on this Vedic culture
like trying to take modern art, Kandinsky,
or physics or Delta Blues

they are all a kind of tuning

far fetched methods
and ways to feel something
about who we are
or maybe a way to fill
the void
        void
old man
                childish shadow

the crick crak of the wind in the dry grass

I am   the leaves
           and the trees
           and the grasses

the wind from past centuries
            at my back
            old old father and mothers
            spirits

it all came upon me

        I was the boy buoy
                          boy or boy
                          oboyo

bobbing around on a sea
of probability
~~~~~~~~~~~~~~~~~~~
~~~waves~~~~~~~~~~~
~~~~~~~~~waves~~~~~~
~~~~~~~~~~~~~~~~~~~

in from past centuries
      toward distant tomorrows

I was the shadow of my old man
now my child is the shadow of me

faces with their eyes like tunnels,
and their mouths like tunnels
and their noses like tunnels,
that go back

faces with their eyes like tunnels
that go back into time.

go back
into our baby time
and home time
and high school time
all that time that makes us up
calcified
and solidified
into heavy mental objects
to which we relate.

our faces are like round clocks,
with the little nose in the middle
(behind the face the idle and escarpment)
 around which the hands move in expressions

and yet that is just a part of the manifold,
this ghost hydra of time tunnels

(You've seen manifolds,
—the intake manifold,
with its many chambered heart,
the carburetor worn on the outside of its sleeve
that leads into valves;

and the exhaust manifold,
with ducting
and long flue
to carry away the dirty air)

but this manifold is more like a mandala maybe
or like a quincunx, or
maybe it's like a jelly fish floating in the wavy sea
```
~~~~~~~~~~~~~~~~~~~~
~~~waves~~~~~~~~~~~~
~~~~~~~~~~waves~~~~~~
~~~~~~~~~~~~~~~~~~~~~

          __
        /    \
      /  ~ ~  \
      \   -  /
       \ __ /
     _\ | /_____            | | |_____/
       / | \                        ` \ _____/
```

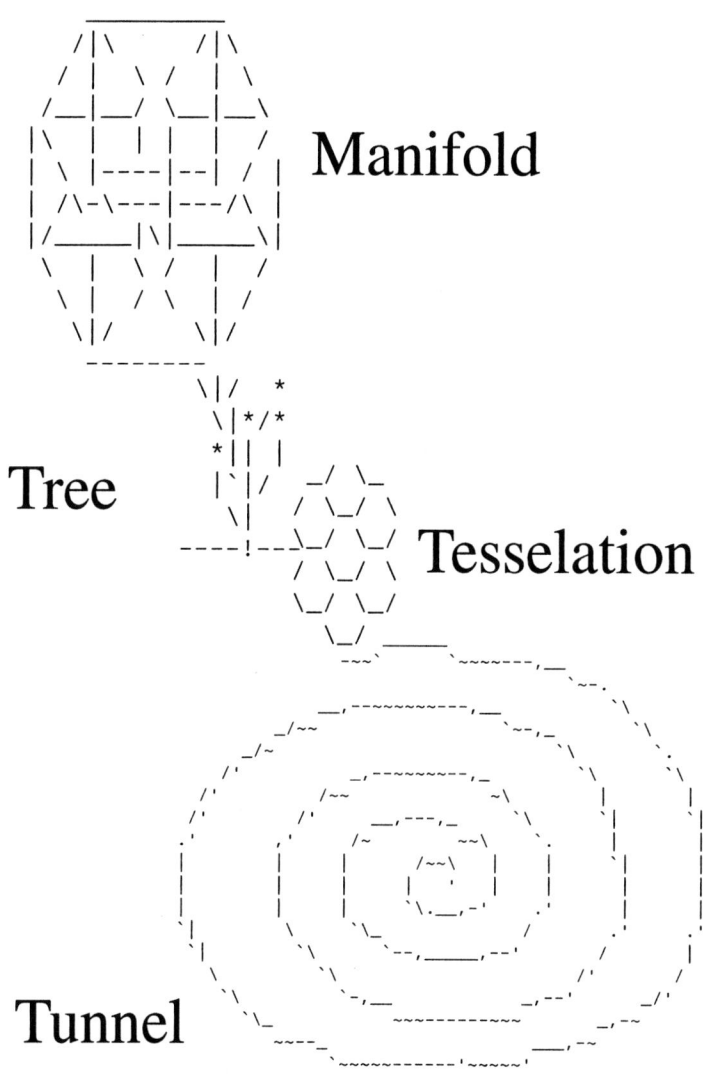

hyperspectral

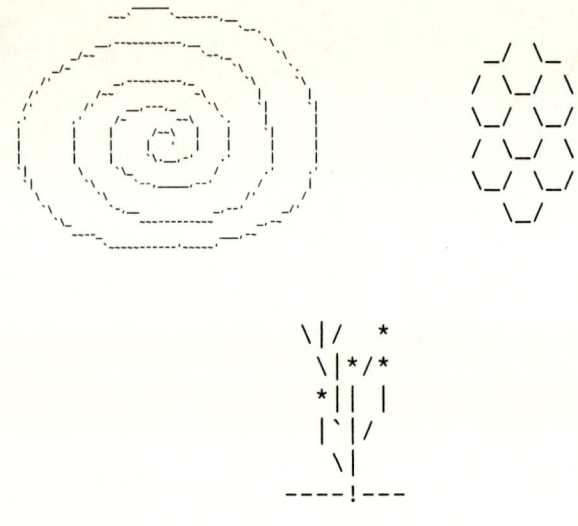

The Secret of the Cicadas' Song

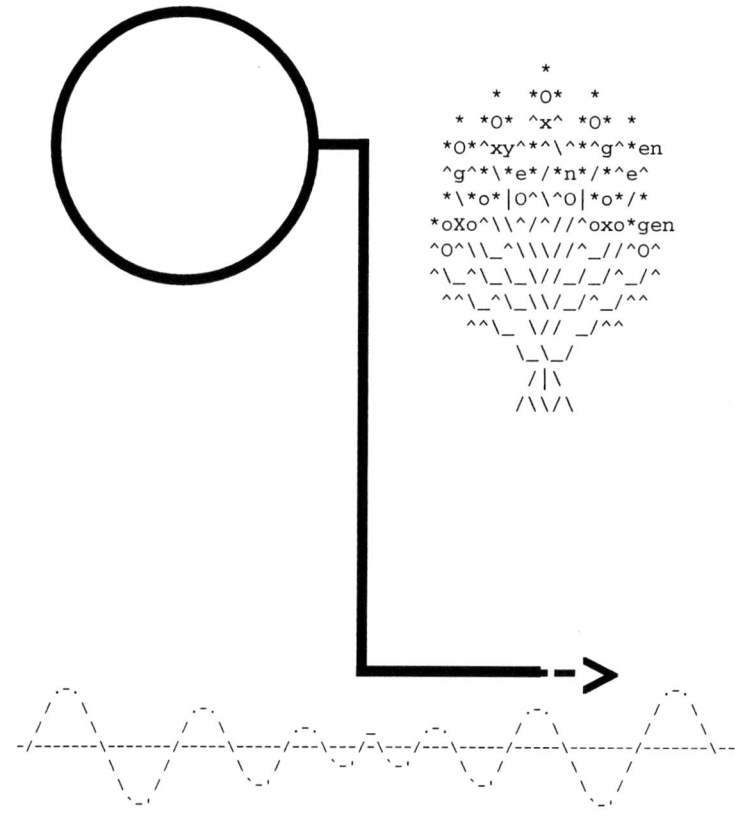

but what my eyes have seen!
other mathematical manifolds, of differential topology,
Klein bottle,
starburst, fractal warp
spaces wild and tame

the rubber geometry of Rieman
the cardioid of Winfree
the discontinuity of Schwartzchild
the toroidal
and other types of hyperspace and time travel

light is the thread
    that weaves together
        space and time

An analogy:
 light is the thread that weaves together space and time,
marriage is the thread that weaves together different families
birth is the thread that weaves together life and time
birth is a big bomb that blows up in the face of entropy
and just as the eye breaks light into its colors
the mind breaks up the universe into its signs

follow the light
    back to the manifold

the warp and weft:
    threads of a tapestry
        and if you look at it for a while
        shapes and patterns
        emerge from this tapestry

we are like atoms around a nucleus,
people sitting at a table talking,

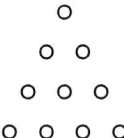

and an electron runs through it,

    —(did you know
    that an electron
    moving
    near the speed of light
    has the mass
    of a greyhound bus)

randomly bumping into tables and knocking guests out of
their chairs and over to other tables

time dilates
length contracts
mass expands
luckily you don't have to
confront relativity on a daily basis

Gaia and the Green Bank

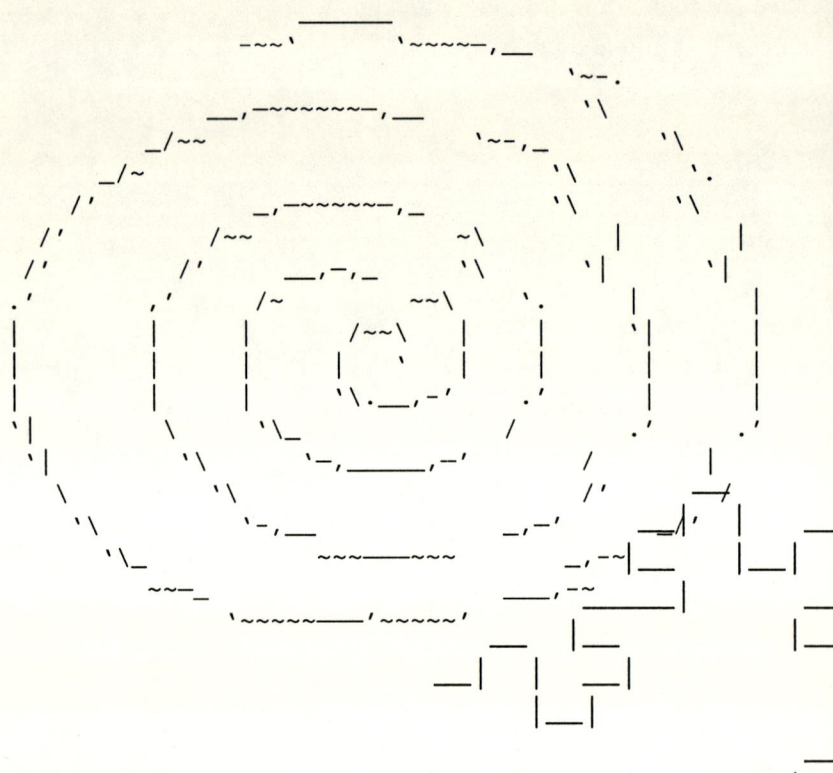

THE PRAIRIE
A vast curving land,
boarded by the hill country to the west
the ground is light brown.
Here and there
planted by farmers around a house,
are clumps of short trees.
the creeks are lined with trees
—a croisenay of fences
separates the champagne fields
from the green pastures
from the dark woods.

leaf feather

    Something
    a dog!
    perhaps, moving
through the forest
    makes
    a covey of birds
    suddenly explode
    from a tree
    and fan out
    everywhere

                            The silence
                            draws back invaded.

     —|
|—
    ——|
|—   a long feather
  —| flits
| flys
                      filters
                            down

                            envied

                            by the tethered
                                      leaves

Green Bank parade

When the white dove sails
into the ground,
and the birds in her flock
leave her to fly away
and it is time
for the warmth in her body
to flow out
and the stillness
which can no longer
be kept at bay
      creeps in.
Then the Green Bank opens
and rocks start divulging their secrets.
The insects begin to scuttle over
from 'neath leaf & borough
to carry her down,
to partake in her energy.
The Green Bank opens
and admits the precious body in parts,
—currency of a spent life.
But the pattern abides.
The efficient activity of these the littlest brethren
is part of the dance
as they partake
in a eucharistic celebration
of the big occasion.
Life's act
is over, once again.

Green Bank as recursive, acausal, semi-permeable membrane

by now I was melting down, not my usual self
it was as if the thousands of bacteria and cells and chemicals
that hold me together had decided to relax into something
more amorphous for a while, and I could sense the horrible
presence that I had been colonized, that many other beings
were living within me, like the way a cold settles into the lungs
in the monsoon season.
I was expiring from lack of oxygen,
meanwhile undergoing metamorphosis

I thought
We may be the last generation to die!
God! No! Not me!
It's not going to happen to me!
On the other hand seems unnatural if you don't.
Got to go back to the Green Bank,
(-the green bank is another name for the manifold)

You want to know about the universe of the Green Bank?
It's right outside your door
—as close as your back yard.

It's not what you think your see.
You think you see this house and the spreading of the plants
in the garden, but it is really a recursive, acausal, semi-perme-
able membrane —a stochastic confabulistic topological

infindibulum, diagonalizing itself in symmetry adaptation to probability nodes of a multidimensional harmonic/vector space.

You enter the Green Bank by dying and becoming part of that "porous killing field where tracking-ingesting and getting-stomped-on rule the day." As you slowly dissolve into the Green Bank you will find a world haunted by the uncanny aspects of fatality and fate ruled by processes and agreements going back to the beginnings of rocks.

But what if the universal space/time manifold really is like the backyard, a **porous** hyper sponge, in which there were pockets of emptiness and strands of conduit filled with time, gravity, electromagnetism, and other fluids. What if looking up at the night sky we were looking up from under ground into a porous recursive, acausal, semi-permeable membrane, interlaced with strands of 'then' time, and tunnel time?

a bit of a bummer

I am stumbling
        stoned,
                become entangled in some branches,
struggle and twist around to get out,
the spindly tree is like some huge insect trying to devour me!
Their branches are like mandibles!
--nodes on their stick like mandibles,
The hollows of the spaces of the tree are like huge eyes!
Huge insects are looking at me
with their malevolent dark eyes,
or their mouths with feelers feeding.
Their barbs are like mandibles of weird insect bushes.
        I thrash about
                yelling
                Get Away!
                        Get Away!
the hollows
    are
    the leading
        tendrils of life
    moving
        into the niches

I have never cared much for bugs
they are just like death
zeroing in on their prey

they're so god damned ugly for one thing

the anthropoids have this pointy mandibles at every joint,
like walking twigs and sticks, really basic models, like some
kind of medieval knight in armor gone berserk from the far
side

the otherness of them!
talk about alien

it said in the book that they come hundreds unearthing themselves out of the ground in a small area of a few yards, and
climb the trees where they break out of their old body,
hope nothing is going to be coming crawling out up out of this
earth!

Good God!
One is eating the head of its mate!

There are so many of them each just like the other, not an
individual among them.
and acre of soil with a population of 50 million or so insects.
Can that be?
The place is just crawling with them.

There are so many of them and so few of us.

I am
watching a bunch of ants
there is a mound of ants just beside where I am sitting, and a
stream of them are coming and going

each face shiny with an exoskeleton exactly like the next one

carrying bits of leaf down into their hole in the ground.

they are feeding some holy humming hive
each has his own duty
some are porters
some are guards
some are builders,
some are trash men

a big beetle is carrying a crumb
he has a big crumb holding it in his mouthparts
he has mouthparts for eating solid food, which is better than
some which vomit acid on their food to d turn it into a liquid
that can be sponged up with its blunt beak. Or worse ones with
a sharp beak that punctures its victim then pumps in saliva that
digests the victim's muscles.. They then can suck in the soup
it has made of the victim's insides, leaving the skin behind like
an empty sack.
I see the hoards all moving in a row
moving along in lock step governed by some genes that got
fixed into place long ago

I am shivering with revulsion

monstrosity
madness mindlessness
the invertebrates
what if they became large and were walking around among us,
they could probably whip dinosaurs,

that would be a fight
between a giant preying mantis and a raptor
a giant beetle and a triceratops

they are incapable of feelings and rational reflection
they'd just walk among us
biting off our heads and sucking out the moisture

ramming a human with a horn
rasping a terrible serrated mandible across the shoulder of a human, slowly taking the arm off.

Yuck!! Let me stop thinking about this stuff!

bug-eyed monsters
    scuttling and wailing among us
huge hairy spiders
slowly going up the sides of our skyscrapers
spiders as big as basketballs
hanging under the eves our houses.
You leave your car out overnight
and a swarm of giant roaches run out and eat the tires off
down to the metal rims!

Or what would it be like to see them play together in a punk rock band; see them wailing away on knobby sitars tambouras or the making mosh pit wooo

A worm as big as a fire hose wends its way through the gutter.

what if we became like them,
hulking mindless drooling killing machines walking the streets
and crashing through our windows

Hey you lousy lawyer
bloodsucking banker
they are so rapacious and don't have a thought for anything but
themselves

and what if these giant invertebrates just barged in on you
anytime of the day or night the way they do now.
you'd have to have screens like iron bars
which they could probably pry off with their great strength

even a little one would fill up your whole shoe
they would just come and go as they please
just like they do now, you can't intercede with them, reason
with them deal with them.

the only good bug is a dead bug is what most people say.

in addition to their monstrousness,
madness and mindlessness
they are so mysterious.
the way they go about things
living on dirt and shit and death
living all in a pile in a hive
swarming over each other
walking in lines.
It's disguzding.

talk about alien
I wonder how we would be if we ever did get to other planets
and the intelligent life form
 turned out to be giant insects.

the spineless kingdom

I mean with the way they proliferate
you couldn't walk the streets.
 Just to go out to the mail box
you'd have to have a flame thrower
and a bazooka.

they'd come at you anyway
        kamikaze dragonfly,
            no sense whatsoever
Yuck!! Please. Pleeaase.
Let me stop thinking about this stuff!

We'd have to train our own,
they are probably not even trainable for Christ sakes.
But suppose we could train one,
a big beetle, say, or a wasp.
"Go over there and get that ant."
We'd have to have our own and get a balance going.
By God that would force us to learn a little ecology.

And the police, they'd all have to be like robocop:
see a big beetle ramming slamming breaking up a citizen, and

robocop would have to go over there and quick with a borer let the fluid out of the beetle.

they have corrugated radiators
antennae
hunter and grasping pincers
snapping barbed tails
        —stingers
    hooked whip
they can throw out a web or net
like gladiators

Mosquitoes
little hairy vampires roaming the air with long straws to stick in your body and suck out the blood

they come out of the ground, fly through the air, drop from structures, swarm

they don't even have skin.
        Aieee!

she, Gaia, when

HEAT
it is completely still
there's not a cloud in the sky
it just goes on and on like an imense swimming pool I could
dive into

an entire planet with no one on it
except for a lowley peon in white
shuffling on the path to the patch
being toyed with by the jeering sneering blearing sun
making everything prickley with heat

i could fall
and call for hours.
no one would come.

minute by minute
I am melting,
my skin is melting off,
the fluides in it draining out slowly,
leaving a transparent shell of a man

the heat is astounding,
      stupifying
it takes your breath away.

GAIA
the first atmosphere was created by volcanoes.
How?
volcanos begat
    the oceans
the ocean begat
    the algae
the algae begat
    the oxygen
and the sky turned blue.

the oxygen and the sun begat
    the protective o-zone
the ozone and the plants
    begat the animals.

Gaia waited and sweated out
the magma flow for
    a billion and a half years
after the magma
then the water condensed out,
the great flood a torrential downpour
 lasting
    only 100,000 years
a short time comparatively
begat the oceans and lakes and it became the water planet

the next atmosphere, the one we have now was created by life
Oxygen, that's what really got things going.

Then, what happened next?
The moon is in just the right
place to tug at the tides
    the intertidal

                        zone
a place where anything must survive
                    waveshock
                        and
                    desication
            and lightning zaps
                    the little tide pools
            and the first amino acids
                    are formed
cell, no cell
            which we carry around
                    inside our elegant meat bags
the moon and the ocean and the lightning begat
the algae
in no time flat, (relatively speaking) she had the basics of life
beginning and flowing with the tide out into the ocean.
first she polluted the ocean green
            with her blue green algae,
she then used
            the algae to pollute the atmosphere blue
                with Oxygen
from that point on life caught on like fire
to breath is to burn
it was an explosion

Oxygen

I am singing and chanting, breathing in an out
the breathing is a great place to put the focus
when the mind is so tumultuous

and I think
most precious oxygen...
where does it come from.
Once upon a time
there was no Oxygen
it had to be generated by life
from chlOrOphyll
 and phOtOsynthesis
came O_2

it drifted up like smOke
it containded the hOpe
fOr life on this planet.

Gaia knOws

from the pOres Of plants
tO the mOuths of babes
it perculated up
and exOtranspirated

```
                    *
             *    *O*    *
          *   *O*  ^x^  *O*   *
         *O*^xy^*^\^*^g^*en
         ^g^*\*e*/*n*/*^e^
         *\*o*|O^\^O|*o*/*
         *oXo^\\^/^//^oxo*gen
         ^O^\\_^\\\//^_//^O^
         ^\_^\_\_\//_/_/^_/^
          ^^\_^\_\\/_/^_/^^
           ^^\_ \// _/^^
              \_\_/
              /|\
             /\\/\
```

Gaia had planned it all along
because the sun hitting on the oxygen
created the high ozone layer
which only protects the earth from the sun.
so we have Gaia using the sun
to protect the earth from the sun.

look for that same efficient cleverness everywhere

the floating brain

it came floating down a river of time,

a river that had its origin in the first eukaryotic cells,
and prokaryotic cells that...
a little dot, really
so tiny
you have to see it under a microscope, ...
that was a big bang actually
only a little bang, a bang that is expanding out
so slowly,
at an evolutionary pace
yet one that would change the face
of this world
and maybe eventually the universe.
No one knows if a meteor from another system carried the starts of life from the stars, or if it was thermophilic and started in the volcanoes and steam vents or if it was autopoetic if it started here in the primordial methane soup crock of newly formed earth struck by lightning, but how it came here and evolved in time to become one of the many civilizations on planets in the great stream of evolution taking place on all the planets,
eyes looking through membranes...
I'm not a semiotician,
I'm an osmosian.
and then I think of Korzbysky and the general semantics of information coming in through levels of abstraction.
each layer may well be a membrane.
hmmm.
and we are floating out

Mushrooms

I recalled how I used to grow mushrooms

I used to buy mycelium off a good doctor in San Antonio. I had a big 10 jar pressure cooker, and I'd inoculate it into sterilized mason jars I used too have a beard in those days and scrubbed it good, and wore a doctors cap over my hair and sprayed the air with Lysol before the transfer to give it the best chance against all the other microbes.
I had plenty of time to look at the spore prints.
Tons of fine powdery brown spores. Apparently they have the ability to become dormant and travel on a astroid or a comet for millions of years.

Is it sad that we have become Homo Abstractus
or is it wonderful.
The word has become object or sign,
the universe has evolved into a semiotic system,
and all signs of things we are here to read.

We must become universal people.

mushrooms give the uncanny ability to find pathways.
if you let it guide you, you will find pathways through.

It is the 5th kingdom and it definitely has some secrets.

while, symbiosis
beyond cohesion in a species or a group, is the interoperability
of different groups,

But what if Wasson is right.
That the very IDEA of divinity first occurred to man after eating mushrooms. Maybe psychedelics have had that big an effect on the evolution of man. They changed him from an ape to a man, and then they changed him from a man to a what. What's the next stage.

Not anything we would know in our lifetime,
but in the long millennia,
maybe we can look into it.
Maybe encoded in the memory of the mushroom is the inspiration and the knowledge of networks and connections to teach us another physics, and about other dimensions through which beings in the galactic civilizations are communicating with each other, now as we speak, and we don't have the proper receiver for it.
We don't even know what channels to look for.
Stella,
      signposts on the road
stellar filaments like mycelia
networking through the universe

The DNA computer

Gaia is always playing, always exploring.
She has a computer,
a hugely-distributed, massively-parallel computer made up of
infinitely many, infinitesimally small
cellular automata.
Did you know that?
The earth mother is a hacker possessed
with unbelievable power,
and no sense of time.
It has this language,
A, T, C, G
She's syncopated like jazz.
The language is made of only 4 letters,
they are the symbols of her program
A T G C A T G CA T G CA T G CA T G CA T G CA T G
G C A T G C A T G CA T G CA T G C A T G C A T G C
She uses this code.. it is a kind of operating system and she
 stores the code in genetic material, in a kind of memory which
can also act as a computation unit.
It's nice stuff it you can get it.
G C T G A T G C A G CA T G C T G C A
CA T G C T G A T C T G A T G CA T

She sets up a problem, like,
give my TRex
               serrated,
                             inward pointing teeth.

Make the little serrations
sticking out of the tooth edge be joined to the tooth
on a pre-stressed circle
so they can take lots of compression
when biting through bone.
Oooohhh, yea. That would be cool.
And she'll set that to computing on her massively parallel
computer, and though it may take millions of years to run the
calculation,
she is doing it on a
much more densely packed computer
orders of magnitude smaller
than the sub micron geometry of chips,
because it is packed in as swarms
starting on the nanometer level,
and going up
from molecular to cell, to organ, to body, to society.
and back down again
Just a little of this genetic material, has far more memory than
all the memory in all the computers ever made or that ever will
be made.

so lets get a sense of
this computer based on genetic material:
It cranks off a program
which is a particular sequence of the language,
A T G C A T G CA T G CA T G CA T G CA T G CA T G
and this causes molecules to form,

and these molecules react with other molecules
in other parts of the massively parallel computer through a vast
network, a manifold of tubes, tunnels and rivers of lines;
they add and combine in various ways,
producing new molecules
whose sequence is the answer,
to the problem,
How?!
She is constantly at play.
Gaia is using life as the medium to solve design problems.
Mandelbrot had all the resources of IBM to help him apreciate
a geometry of nature. Gaia has the all the resources of the
planet at her disposal to create the interlocking objects of
Nature.

Again, lets get a sense of the scale here:
just a little bit of this genetic material set calculating
would produce more computations
than all the computers ever built.
Because it is a million times smaller than chips.
Now set this computer calculating for millions and millions of
years and look at the result.

that is the green bank, this immense parallel computer

The Green Bank
is all about getting
       and holding energy

look at that bird zooming down so sleek
sharp beak aerodynamic to cut the flow
    feather ailerons,
The bird is a fin-stabilized arrow
for drag reduction
and to conserve energy.

Gaia is constantly at play in the
watercourse way, designing energy flow control.
It is based on previous experiments
the flotsam in the flow:
    whirligig leafs
        gyrate
            and helicopter
back down to mother earth below

thousands of cicadas and crickets and frogs
are singing their music and it is all mixed together
into the rarefactioning drone spreading out all around.
And I get sense of it as I listen into it
of... that they are
singing in the ancient language of insects
a dialect of the language of Gaia.

I think to myself that it's as if I too am a thought
in this great "mind,"
for surely a computer that can think all this into existence
is a mind.

where does language begin / the real name of water

pools of pep in the tides
poly peptides

pools of nucleotides
poplynucleotides

Where does language begin?
At the level of water.

We make the analogy between language and life:
the word is monomer
        sometimes a misnomer
the letters are sugars,
the sentence is a nucleotide, —a concatenation of monomers.
These sentences twist around and come back on themselves,
like that ancient question —
who made me and how long do I have.
The paragraph is the cell
the story is the tissue, the organ
the book is the person.

If a person is a book,
then what are the trees?
that make up leaves of the book.
What are we really looking at
when we are looking at a tree?

When I say the word tree,
it conjures up only the abstraction tree,
that marvelous branching structure,
upon which is based heredity,
evolution, architecture, lightning cascades, and language.
When we make an analogy or a metaphor it is because there is
this tree-like bifurcating taxonomy underlying everything!
I want to go where that is,
that source of the richness of metaphor.

It happened when I looked at the tree on psychedelics, and saw
not so much the branches and parts of the tree, but the matrix in
which the tree was imbedded and from which it emerges
— that which told the tree
Don't grow here
      branch out
           grow over there.
It is probably something very simple,
some simple rule of grammar, or syntax,
or transformational form.
I never know which is which.

Now, when I say Oak, I think about the family of all oak trees,
the trees that remember oakness in their history, and whose
lives can be rolled all into a ball in the tinniest acorn and past
on to grow for another lifetime.
It remembers its own history in
the ocean of nucleotides

a sea which I am swimmin' in
bobbing around on a sea
of probability

~~~~~~~~~~~~~~~~~~~

~~~waves~~~~~~~~~~~

~~~~~~~~~~waves~~~~~~

~~~~~~~~~~~~~~~~~~~

I am a carrier of forms going back millions
and millions of years.
What is the source.
Well, OK,
So suppose there is this field, this intergalactic life field.
What would be its field equations
f (N^o, P, l_z, l, l_i, t_c)
whose solution is the real name of water

$$\omega \Pi \int te^{r(\wp)}$$

what are its parameters, its control entities,
the bodies that govern it,
what are the rules here,
we want to change the way we look at the world.
where
ω   is for angular velocity of curling vorticity fluxes
Π   is the permutation operator looks at all possible avenues the water can go
∫,   is an integral for smoothing
t,   is time
$e^{r(\wp)})$
    is the rate of the exponential expansion flow in time and other dimensions

And suppose we assign three specialists to study it.
One is from the structural school, one from the informational
school and the third from the biochemical school.
They wait for a sign
and soon enough it emerges

hyperspectral

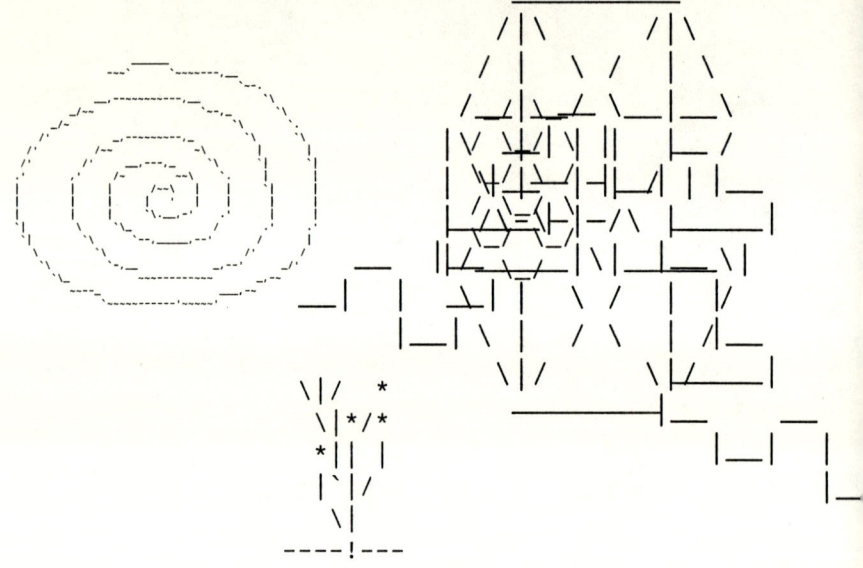

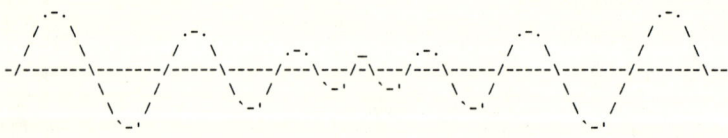

They look at it from different sides, with one eye,
close up, for almost an hour.

"is a kind of space ship, "
"it looks like a tetrahedron,
floating over the ocean, "
"it is a kind of solar sailer,
a huge galleon ghost ship
floating above the waves"
"a tetrahedronal life form "
"the origin of signs "

and the biochemestry guy says "Let us try to get a picture
of this mystical body as it composes itself,
in the small unused dimension
within membrane with membrane within membrane
communication percolating and transporting over surfaces.

call it an endoplasmic reticulum
call it an ectoplasmic rediculum

And the geometry guy, the structuralist school says
"...a space time manifold composed itself
and we say these dimensions allow form
—the most basic kind of communication —"

"Yes," interupted the 2nd one from the biochemical school,
"they are communicating by accretion, solution,..."

"or more basic: code translation," said the 2nd one, from the
Information school,
 "They are cellular automata tiling the plane.
It projects space and time as a particular
tiling of the surface in 4-dimensional space/time..."

"...cellular automata are quasi-crystals"

"...quasi-crystals ? what is that you qwazie rabbit,"
It has sensitivity, memory, this medium.
This water,
And it was automorphic,
the automorph emerges,

floats over the water
rises up out of the water,
and this Automorph
began to play in the fields of molecules and cells,
pools of pep in the tides
poly peptides
pools of nucleotides
poplynucleotides

The Water Automorph
flowed in and around
began to play in the fields of molecules and cells,
and applied its techniques of allurement,
accretion
       and solution.
its effluvial techniques of
       mass transfer,
              chemical reaction,
                     mixing/separating,
                            diluting/concentrating,
                                  thinning/thickening the flow,
creating turbulence,
vorticity fluxes, pressure-gradient flows,
       viscosity-gradient flows ,
              suction/injection,
                     dispersing, diffusing,
                            heating/cooling,
       cavitation,
       sublimation,
influencing, shaping, to name a few.

And this Automorph brought forth the millions of life forms,
Water is the skin on the mystical body of earth.
Life emerges from the water
"we have
      we have
            tall
      we have tall lifeforms
      the lifeforms aligning themselves in a protean stream,"
said the biochemist,
"they are all afloat on their niche,"
"...and they don't notice what goes on in other niches," said
the information theorist, "because that information is not of
immediate need or use."
The cellular automata Automorph is signaling as well as being
a bit of structure as well as holding something in memory. Now
that is good, we have the structuralists, the informationists, and
a biochemist there holding a place in time (memory)
—three parts to every sign.
The information is the energy transfer.
The structural is the purely geometrical, -- this has to do with
complying to the laws of physics which are themselves expressions of symmetries.
And the biochemical gets down to the actual physical elements
or units we are dealing with.
In terms of signage Peircean,
the age old question of how man is to fit in this
is answered:
to not get in the way,
—not that you could.

Green Bank formula

so what is in this green bank formula anyway
$f(N^O, P, l_z, l, l_i, t_c) = (N^*) \times (fP) \times (nLZ) \times (fL) \times (fI) \times (FC)$
we're all in the green bank formula,

The Green Bank Formula is the probabilities of our lives,
that we might reach a level of intelligence and be able to
communicate to other intelligent beings.
We are all trying to be intelligent life forms
trying to communicate out of our little sphere

the stillness is not empty
it is filled with potential in a tenuous equilibrium

So, (N^*) the star, would be the first to cleave space
and make light in the darkness,
and that it would be a steady state thing for a long time,

And that there would be parts of itself,
(fP), is the probability that planets would fragment off
that had not accreted or had been blown off,
that orbited around it, stayed in the family,
and one or more of these would turn out to have life.

(nLZ), would express this
—the number of planets in a life zone.

We are time averages
over the ebb and flow of neuropeptides
the foam and ferment of enzymes
and the first part (N*) x (fP) x (nLZ) is
the probability that a matrix will develop for life to swarm.

(fL) is the probability that life will originate if conditions are suitable —this we can assume is 1, we know it to be a certainty.

(fI) is the probability of technological intelligent life will evolve and

(FC) is the fraction of a star's life during which the life form is communicative.

N = (N*) x (fP) x (nLZ) x (fL) x (fI) x (FC)
is a model of, and a way to do an estimate calculation of the number of planets with intelligent life forms out there.

There must be others out there.
How would you recognize this?
Well there ought to be some kind of signal...
We think there ought to be some kind of a life field that shows itself, but since it is molecular and electromagnetic its signal would fall of as the distance squared.

We need to look at something on the macro scale,
an increase in entropy.

An overall increase in entropy as the sign of life?
Yes, life evolving toward higher complexity plays out entropy's plan, because organisms of higher complexity create more entropy. Part of that evolutionary thrust toward higher complexity is the universe trying to know itself. The question is how would the universe knowing itself,
that is to say being able to predict and control better,
lend itself to furthering the goals of higher entropy.
Well, of course, a long lived complex organism who itself was able to create even more complex organizations, would best further the goals of entropy.

How would we measure that.
$S = k \log (W)$
entropy is proportional to the logarithm of the energy density or inversely
$e^S = k^{-1} W$
an increase in energy density cause an exponential increase in entropy.
If you have something creating more energy density,
it also creates more entropy.

yes zooming down into this matrix whence we come
in powers of e,
yes that would be cool.

where we will be getting to is through,
from the exponentiation
of these realms.

Wow that sounds like the production of an artist, the probability that he will survive free and be able to continue creating, or get locked up into a job, the probability that he will find a way to get access to media, to become the person of our dreams and finally how long can you keep some kind of horrendous creative block from coming down, how long can you keep communicating.

We would look for water —sure
what does its spectra look like.
Amorphous, no sharp lines.
There must be some telltale perfectly exact signature of water that we can look for.

they wanted to be able to start calculating *ab initio*
an *aufbau* of species filling each niche
you could predict where a niche would be and how it would be filled by looking at the hydrodynamic control issues involved.

Start with the hypergeometric equation
$f(N^o, P, l_z, l, l_i, t_c)$
on an infinite dimensional Hilbert space,
that's a good place to start.

Green Bank Definition

the green bank:
nature invests
in the long run.
for in the long
run, much
more entropy
gets produced
by a big, long-lived,
smart mammal
going round
digging tunnels,
and blasting
Panama Canals,
and creating more and more
big long-lived smart manipulators
making it possible
to produce way more
entropy.
higher organization
produces more
entropy...
Order
is the interest
that entropy pays
in units of information
for the use of energy.

the heart is a strange attractor

I was feeling these rushes in the heavy heat,
a heat so heavy you could float in it.
My heart was doing flip, flops,
I thought it was gonna jump outa my chest.

I'd been going for days on this idea of fractals and chaos,
the story about how mother nature extracts chaos and order out
of randomness and noise,
that's the story of our time.
To be able to understand that,
and to know that
and to know how we are all a part of that,
is what I wanted.

hey, but enough about me.
what about you.
How's your heart?

The heart you've got one you know,
best machine ever invented by nature
holds a special place in the museum of mechanical marvels.

And once you know that
you'll never be able to go back to Babylon, to the wasteland,
of the cubicles and the job and same old married life,
you have to get the fear and get moving,
get moving you know.

and what if we looked at the economy and found that it really
is pretty much a self-regulating system and that all these
politicians and bureaucrats are not necessary.

I was stuck out there in the heat
and was being sucked down
into the ultimate attractor nature ever made
the heart, seat of the 5th element —love,

heart agape chaos
path with heart.
What is the heart anyway.

What *AM* I doing here.
Came out here for a season, sweated out the summer in Texas
and what have I got to show for it.

I'm getting these rushes getting short of breath,
each one might be my last,
getting more and more filled with fear and dread,
sweating it out,
as the world is divulging to me some ultimate secret.
The heart is a strange attractor.
It is the seat of the 5th element —Love.
It is about to beat out of this chest!
ba bump
babababababababab (stop freeze)
palpitations?

I'd be out there looking at the weather looking at the sky,
looking to see if there are cells and circulations but it is a
completely abstract space a space that you can only see with
your imagination,

lub lub lub dub
tachycardia?
but this being inside the heart was a more physical space that
actually used the audio depth perception of the brain,
the way it localized sound in space, by noting the difference
between phases in the signals.

It's probably just
gas and that burning sensation.
Heart ache.
There are all sorts of arrhythmias, blockages and weaknesses.

just as long as it's not fibrillation
that's the worst of all —fibrillation.
that's when just enough current goes into the heart to get it to
oscillate wildly, to beat out of the chest.
this eventually leads to the steady state of death.
flat-lined

don't think about your heart.
you can't not think about your heart
because
the heat is a microcosm of the world

close up you'd hear the wooshings and pounding of fluid against fluid, fluid against solid and solid against solid. Blood courses from chamber to chamber, squeezed by the contracting muscles behind and then stretches the walls ahead. Fibrous valves snap shut audible against the backflow. The muscle contractions themselves depend on a complex three-dimensional wave of 'lectrical activity.

phase locked muscle cells
some of which sit out the dance for a turn or two
to get a rest
where did nature learn to construct such a thing.
nature modeled and modeled the heart over and over again in species until she found one that worked.

or the immune system
things are no longer even remotely crystalline and Pythagorean.

The Background Hiss of Summer

"The background hiss of summer, the background hiss of summer," I kept thinking, against the complex texture of bright summer grasses, shot through with bursts and buzzes of white noise shaped by crickets and cicadas. I did the snake shuffle, boots dragging along the ground sending out plenty of snake warning vibrations and crackling through dried reeds.

I had become acclimatized to the country. I wore loose white cotton and a big wide brimmed Panama hat made of loose weave straw. I had more of a body awareness. If a tick or any insect got on me, I could immediately sense it and gracefully, absent-mindedly remove the critter. Being always alert for snakes, led to a kind of enhanced awareness of the environment. This simplified life of hauling water and tending plants, and the intense heat seemed to slow time down somehow. I had become increasingly alert to the marijuana world, the kind of alertness, as they say in the *Tao Te Ching*, that is necessary to the mastery of a subject.

God damn! It is hot. Every day in the high nineties and low 100s. There was a terrible drought in Texas and we really had to stay on top of the watering. At least until hurricane season.

The background hiss of summer.

Yes

The background hiss of summer rises with heat.

If you listen in to it, into the cicadas, what you get are these layers of silence and sound that seem to travel. Walls of noise that are thrown up, then vanish with an abruptness that is so sudden that your mind keeps on going like a vector into silence. It's like when you look out onto the road and see the heat rising in wavering undulating columns. Like a mirage, the heat makes the landscape shift and move through a lens of air. You could actually feel the shifting of the microclimate, the movement of the heat. But now the mirage of heat was actually being translated by the cicadas into a wavering and shifting in the wall of sound, in the cosmic buzz moving through all things. It was like the cosmic buzz, —the heat permeating the universe, left over from the explosion of the big bang — was a fundamental and all the things that lived up and down the order of heat niches were harmonics of this background heat buzz. A kind of biological *aufbau*, orbital filling. The ever widening circles of matter circulating around smaller circles, quarks around energy, electrons around neutrons, molecules around atoms, cells around molecules, organs around cells, beings around organs, families around beings, communities around families, ever expanding outward chains of being like a pebble dropped into pond.

Are the cicadas attuned to the cosmic buzz? I asked myself. What do they know of the cosmic buzz?! It's as if the insects and plants are saying, "I've got a secret."

So I began to do drugs and wander the fields and take dictation from the background hiss of summer. —pretty crazy out there,

I have pulled together some of the experiences in a long poem-like entity called Hyperspectral/the Dirac Satori.

I had a lot of time on my hands that summer and I started exploring concrete poetry on the typewriter.

I also got these ideas about trying to write about the Satori. Seemed like that was a worthwhile subject. The satori I experienced while on peyote and other psychedelics, and sometimes while not on drugs. Satori is a philosophical moment, in which you feel your presence in the universe.

The poem would start out with the narrator, the I wanting to understand the archetypes of perception that I was seeing in the psychedelic.

I started off with some kind of philosophical quest, to know something of the transcendental reality we all have a right to know at the basis behind the chatter, I started off with the desire of a physics student at that time, — the first generation to grow up with a readily excepted view of relativity, and quantum mechanics, and hyper-spaces — but mainly I began to want to write a poem that was about perception and about the idea of word as object, like the way that we see through a narrator's view as a kind of word as programming the human computer to see. And of course that lead to notation.

Word as object is notation. But even more than that I wanted to have a poem that gave a world view of someone that was slowed down and walking through the forest and starting to see the web of life, or the semiotics of symbiosis.

So I conceived of a poem which had a narrator, but the narrator maybe shifted to Gaia being the narrator, or the narrator emphasizing with Gaia. But it was something that was much bigger than Gaia, I called it Noo-sphere first spoken about in Tieard de Chardin. But that hasn't been updated and it came to me that a structure might be the Green Bank, well it would be a kind of seed bank and it was in the parameters of the Green Bank formula that I got a picture of this hyperspectral aspect of communication to the physical spectral. I also wanted to find a more ancient basis for it in the Vedas, which is to say in the origin of grammar as a way of structuring reality.

I'd sit there at my typewriter and take dictation from the waves of cicada rising and falling and I wrote this narrative poem. *

And in writing that poem I came to know their secret! The song of the grasshoppers is a harmonic of the white noise left over by the big bang!

"That's the secret of the Grasshopper's trilling!" I shouted aloud to nobody in particular.

"The background hiss of summer, is crickets and grasshoppers stridulating, looking for the resonance frequency of summer, so that they can drive it, to create a message that gets transmitted through the leftover ubiquitous background heat radiation of the universe and travel quickly to other planets."

Yes. That's it.

Do you think there can be any truth to that?

I've got to tell somebody, anybody, her. Got to tell Ruth.

Yeah Rrrright. I could see myself telling her.

HiT MoteL Press

www.hitmotel.com

These books can be ordered from any book seller or on-line .
Check www.hitmotel.com for selections and recordings.

Boho Novels
The Little House on the Prairie Trilogy:
Cultivating the Texas Twister Hybrid, a portrait of the artist as a weed gardener (1998) ISBN 0-9655842-0-8 $20.00
The Secret of the Cicadas' Song, a peyote trip in poetry and prose (1998) ISBN 0-9655842-1-6 $20.00
Knight of 1000 eyes, about Tai Chi, movement, Laban, and the I Ching (1998) ISBN 0-9655842-2-4 $20.00

The Punctual Actual Weekly, about the life and times of a small mimeograph literary rag centered around artists living in a Berkeley warehouse and the Amphictionic Theatre (2000) ISBN 0-9655842-8-3
The Church of the Coincidental Metaphor, youthful adventures in Mexican radio   ISBN 0-9655842-7-5
The Indigenous Tribesmen of Neverland, bohemian life in Austin slacker enclaves (1999) ISBN 0-9655842-6-7 $20.00
Sex is the Anti-gravity of Metamorphosis, tales of romance and despair hitchhiking in US, Canada and Mexico. (1999) ISBN 0-9655842-9-1

Novels:
My Years of Apprenticeship at Love Trilogy:
Dolores Park, Texan joins a California Tantric Buddhist commune (1999) ISBN 0-9655842-3-2 $20.00
The Jung of University Avenue, a journal of psychotherapy (1999) ISBN 0-9655842-4-0
A Blue Moon in August, about marriage and children late in life. (1999) ISBN 0-9655842-5-9

CD-ROM
Cultivating the Texas Twister Hybrid CD-ROM, radio plays of actor's voices performing bits from the novels, the Mirage Symphony

Nonfiction
The Diamond Cutter's Sutra, about semiotics, logic, semantic object modeling, mathematics --a kind of Varieties of Logical Experience

Check into HiT MoteL chat and framed presentation about emergent complexity constantly drifting through. @www.hitmotel.com

Check out this audio CD from **HiT MoteL** Press

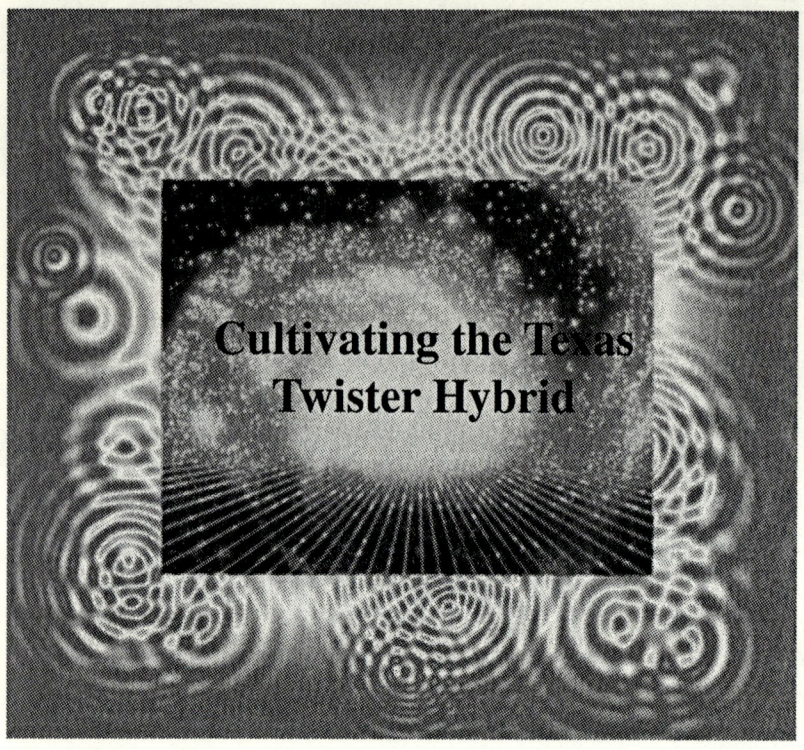

Cultivating the Texas Twister Hybrid

Set against the music of storms, winds, and the natural environment of cicadas, crickets, frogs and birds these radio plays enacted by voice-over actors speaking lines from novels by Michael Lyons present a very special 3D sound experience. In particular the Mirage Symphony shows how a symphonic structure imbues the ambient sounds of the world, indicating a dialog or a thought in the universal mind.

Catman in Dogwalk House
Loafers of the Kandinsky Sound Museum
The Background Hiss of Summer
Stockhausen
Somtimes He'd Dance at Night
Caterwalling at the Speed of Light
The Mirage Synphony
Oxygen
Green Bank Parade

You can read the script and listen to samples from the radio play on the website at

www.hitmotel.com

HiT MoteL Press

presents these other books in the series by Michael Lyons

Cultivating the Texas Twister Hybrid is the first book. It is about the adventures of a city guy on a farm growing weed. It is a gardener's journal teaching the growers craft and something of the connoisseurs's educations as well as a criminal's internal monolog.

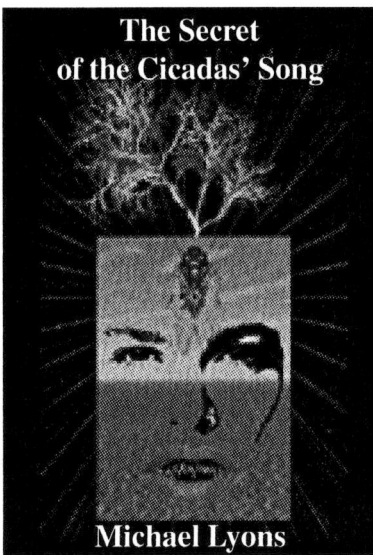

The Secret of the Cicadas' Song is another books about an event on the farm. It is an extended peyote trip in prose and poetry. The time of the book is a peyote trip. One is brought to the immediacy of the experience through haiku poetry and to the ineffable aspect of the experience through object verse and semantic object modeling of the archetypes of perception.

Knight of 1000 eyes is another books about an event on the farm. The time of the book is a tai chi session. It reflects the struggle of the western mind coming to understand the spirit of the universe. It has an essay on western space time motion philosopher Laban and a modern commentary on the ancient I Ching.

www.hitmotel.com

to order directly from HiT MoteL by Mail go to the website and
1. Print this form.
2. mail this form with check or money order (made out to Michael Lyons) to:

HiT MoteL Press
2267 28th Ave.
San Francisco CA 94116

Name:_____

Address:_____

City:_____State:_____Zip:_____

Telephone:_____E-mail:_____

Title: Cultivating the Texas Twister Hybrid
ISBN 0-965542--0-8   @: $20 Qty:_____   Total:$_____

Title: The Secret of the Cicadas' Song
ISBN 0-965542--1-6   @: $20 Qty:_____   Total:$_____

Title: The Knight of 1000 eyes
ISBN 0-965542--2-4   @: $20 Qty:_____   Total:$_____

The Texas Twister CD-ROM
                      @: $20 Qty:_____   Total:$_____

                                Sub Total:$_____
                CA residents please add 8%:_____
                                Shipping:_____
                             Grand Total:_____

Shipping Information:
Shipping - Please add $3.50 for first item, $1.00 for each additional item
We ship via US Priority mail or UPS.

The Secret of the Cicadas' Song

The Secret of the Cicadas' Song is an extended internal monolog of a man walking through the fields on peyote.

Through semantics, semiotics, logic, fractals, chaos theory, sound, haiku, symbols, archetypes etc. the poem induces, a swooning nominal neumenal drug experience. We are present while the consciousness of the poem constructs various notation systems as the words in his language become objects.

One generative hypothesis of the poem is:

What would happen if Ezra Pound and Charles Dodson collaborated about being influenced by Wittgenstein, Hilbert, Dirac, Mandelbrot, Basho, Burroughs, Borges, Bukowski, Cendrars, Saunders...

The time of the book is a peyote trip. One is brought to the immediacy of the experience through haiku poetry and to the ineffable aspect of the experience through object verse and semantic object modeling of the archetypes of perception. The point of view shifts from the individual consciousness to the mind of Gaia.

$20.00 Literature / Philosophy / Poetry / Peyote
The HiT MoteL Press   http://www.hitmotel.com